The Riddle of the Hollow Tree

Enid Blyton

The Riddle of the Hollow Tree

AWARD PUBLICATIONS LIMITED

This book was first published in Great Britain under
the title *Hollow Tree House* by The Lutterworth Press
in 1945. It was updated and altered to become part
of the Riddle series in 1997 by Enid Blyton's
daughter, Gillian Baverstock.

For further information on Enid Blyton
please visit *www.blyton.com*

ISBN 978-1-84135-740-9

Illustrated by Patricia Ludlow
Cover illustration by Gavin Rowe

Illustrations copyright © Award Publications Limited

First published 1945 as *Hollow Tree House*
Revised edition published 1997 as *The Riddle of the Hollow Tree*
First published by Award Publications Limited 2004 as
The Young Adventurers and the Hollow Tree
This edition entitled *The Riddle of the Hollow Tree*
first published 2009

Published by Award Publications Limited,
The Old Riding School, The Welbeck Estate,
Worksop, Nottinghamshire, S80 3LR

12 3

Printed in the United Kingdom

CONTENTS

CHAPTER 1

CROSS AUNT MARGARET

Nick and Katie stood outside the kitchen door of their home and listened. From inside came the sound of a scolding voice.

"You've sat in that chair and slept for two whole hours, you lazy wretch! You get outside and mend that shed door!"

"She's in a bad temper again," said Nick, frowning. "Listen to her! It's no good asking her today."

The children walked down the garden and sat on a pile of logs. Nick was twelve and Katie was just eleven. It was easy to see that they were brother and sister, for they had the same dark brown eyes and straight brown hair. Katie looked at Nick.

"If we don't ask Aunt Margaret tonight, we shan't be able to go on the school trip," she said. "We've got to take the money to Mrs Hall tomorrow. We're the only ones who haven't paid yet."

"I hate having to ask her for money," said Nick. "If only Mum and Dad were still here they'd have paid for the school trip, knowing we'd have a marvellous time."

Six months before, Nick and Katie had lost both their parents in a car crash just after Christmas. Their grandmother was too badly injured in the accident to be able to care for the children, so their neighbours had looked after them for the first few weeks while their future was decided. Great-aunt Jill was too old to help. Uncle Bob, their father's best friend, and Uncle Charlie, their mother's brother, were their guardians. It had been decided that the two children should go to live with Uncle Charlie and his wife, Aunt Margaret.

"I wish we could have gone to live with Uncle Bob," said Katie sadly. "He's such fun and he wouldn't have treated us unkindly like Aunt Margaret does."

"He couldn't look after us because detectives work all hours," said Nick, who was Uncle Bob's godson and admired him tremendously. "And anyway, he's been sent to Australia for three years."

"Uncle Charlie's all right," said Katie,

"but he's so scared of Aunt Margaret that he never says anything when she's angry and scolds us."

"And now that Uncle Charlie's lost his job, she'll be unbearable," said Nick gloomily. "I wish we could have lived with Mike and Penny next door. Their mum and dad were so kind those first awful weeks after the crash."

"I know, but there wasn't any room for us there after their grandmother went to live with them," said Katie. "We were lucky Mr and Mrs Fraser agreed to let Mike and Penny look after Punch when we couldn't take him to Aunt Margaret's."

"I still can't bear to think about him," said Nick. "He was the best dog in the world."

The two children looked unhappily at each other. Everything was so very different from a year ago: no Mum and Dad, no pets, no excitement, and nothing to look forward to. The school trip would be such fun but if Aunt Margaret was in a bad temper, she wouldn't let them go.

"Everyone else in the school is going, simply everyone," said Katie. "A whole day by the sea! Think of it! And it's not as if it's an expensive trip."

"I know. I wish we had the money, then we could go without asking Aunt Margaret," said Nick. "We never have pocket money, though I'm sure we're meant to have some from the money Uncle Bob sends for our keep. It's only when Uncle gives us something on the sly that we have anything to spend. And then, if Aunt Margaret finds it, she takes it away!"

They stopped talking for a moment and listened to the scolding voice that still came out from the open kitchen door.

"Sitting there with the newspaper in front of you all day long! Lost your job again – and no wonder! The only thing you're ever on time for is your meals. What with you to look after, and your tiresome nephew and niece, I'm just about fed up!"

There was a loud thump as Aunt Margaret spoke. She was ironing, and the children could tell by the bangs of the iron what a bad temper she was in.

They waited for a while. Then their uncle came out with a sulky look on his face. He caught sight of the two children.

"One of these days I shall walk right out of the house and never come back!" he said to them. "There's no peace in this place at all! Nag, nag, nag, all day long."

"Uncle, I suppose you couldn't possibly let us have some money, could you?" said Nick rather hopelessly, for when his uncle had no job, he usually had no money either.

"Money! Whatever for?" asked Uncle Charlie.

"To go on the school trip," said Katie eagerly. "You remember. You signed the form for us to say we could go."

"I haven't any for myself, let alone for you!" said her uncle, dipping his hands into his pockets. He brought up a few pence, and that was all. "Your aunt takes all she can get. Better ask her!"

He went off down the lane, and the children watched him. He was an engineer and had once run his own business, but things had gone wrong and he had been forced to sell it. He hated working for other people and was always in trouble for being careless or arriving late.

Suddenly their aunt came to the door and saw them. "What are you idling out there for?" she called out in her usual sharp voice. "Katie, come on in and help me with the ironing. Nick, tidy up the shed. If you think I'm going to let you grow up as lazy as your uncle you're wrong."

That wasn't a fair thing to say, because neither Nick nor Katie was lazy. They were working hard at school and Katie had won the story-writing prize that term. At home they did plenty of odd jobs for their aunt, and did them well.

Katie went indoors with a sigh. It was hot, and ironing would make her feel hotter still. Nick went to the untidy shed where his uncle's dirty tools lay on the floor. Uncle Charlie could never be bothered to hang them up.

In the kitchen, Aunt Margaret was still in a bad temper. Katie said nothing. She began putting the pressed clothes neatly in a basket. She did her best, hoping that Aunt Margaret would feel pleased with her. Then perhaps she might ask her aunt if they could go on the school trip.

Nick came back in. He stood near Katie, wondering if he dared to ask for the money for the trip.

"What are you doing standing there?" said his aunt sharply. "Want to get something out of me, I suppose! Well, what is it?"

Aunt Margaret was clever at reading people's thoughts. Nick knew he would have to ask her now.

"You see, Aunt, it's the school trip tomorrow and Mrs Hall is taking us all to

the sea for the day," he began. "The tickets include our tea as well. It's not a lot. We have to take our own lunch. Everybody else is going, so Katie and I wondered if we could go too."

Thump, thump, went the iron angrily, and Nick's heart sank.

"And where are you going to get the money from?" asked his aunt.

"Well, we thought perhaps you could spare it just this once," said Nick.

THUMP, went the iron. And then Aunt Margaret began one of her angry tirades. "You thought I could spare it! With your feckless uncle out of work again! And me working hard in that village shop to make money to keep all four of us! You ought to be ashamed to ask, Nick, and you too, Katie!"

Nick opened his mouth to speak, but his aunt swept on, banging the iron down at the end of each sentence.

"It was a bad day for me when I married that lazy uncle of yours! And what does he do when his sister dies but brings you here and tells me it's our duty to look after you! 'Both their parents dead, poor little orphans. We've no children of our own, Margaret,' he says, 'so we'll do our best to care for them!' And then he's too lazy to keep a job!"

"Aunt Margaret," began Nick, "it was kind of you to take us in, but there's money for you to spend on our clothes and keep and things. Uncle Bob said there was."

Thump thump thump! Aunt Margaret snorted as she ironed.

"It takes a great deal of money to buy you both everything you need, and your Uncle Bob only sends money every three months. It's run out now and the next lot's not due for another fortnight," said Aunt Margaret crossly.

"Uncle Bob told me there should be enough money to last until we are both grown-up," said Nick bravely. "If you run out before the three months are up, can't you write to him and explain that we both had to have new school uniforms this term?"

"And have him say I'm being extravagant – or using it for myself?" shouted Aunt Margaret as she banged the iron down. "I don't know why your uncle brought you here, when you could have gone into care. I never liked children and I didn't want you, but I've got to put up with you. So don't you come asking me for money for school trips!"

Katie was crying. "Don't keep saying you don't want us," she sobbed. "It's awful not to be wanted. I'm glad you didn't let us go into care. We do try to help you all we can."

"Oh, go out of doors if you're going to cry all over the ironing," said her aunt impatiently, but she looked a little ashamed of herself. Katie slipped out at once, and Nick followed her.

They went out of the gate and crossed to the wood that stretched for some miles over the countryside. They sat down on a bank of grass and Nick put his arm round Katie.

"Don't cry, Katie," he said. "What's the use? We know Aunt Margaret doesn't want us, but at any rate she gives us a home."

"It's not a proper home," said Katie, wiping her eyes. "Proper homes aren't like this. Think of our old home, Nick – or Mike and Penny's, or Laura's."

Nick thought of their old home, and of their parents, who had never minded how much time and trouble they took with them both.

Katie remembered how her mother loved to hear about what she'd done at school and how delighted her father was when she'd got her bronze medal for swimming. They would both have been so pleased to know that she'd come top of her new class.

"Why did Mum and Dad have to die, Nick?" she asked, beginning to cry again.

"I don't know," said Nick, hugging her. "But at least we've got each other. It would be dreadful to live here all alone."

"I couldn't bear it without you," said Katie miserably. "But I want our own home back with Mum and Dad there still."

"Katie, you know that's impossible," said Nick sadly. "I'd give anything to be back with them too, but that can't happen. We've just got to take care of each other."

"If only we could have had Punch with us," said Katie, wiping away another tear.

"Don't let's talk about him. I miss him dreadfully still," said Nick. "At least we know he's well looked after, and Laura does let us share Russet."

CHAPTER 2

MONEY FOR THE SCHOOL TRIP

The sound of someone singing a pop song came through the woods. Katie wiped her eyes for the last time and sat up straight.

"That's Laura," she said. "I recognise her voice."

A girl a little younger than Katie came down the path towards them. She was very pretty with deep blue eyes and fair silky hair down to her shoulders.

"Hello, Katie, hello, Nick!" she called. "I wondered if I should see you today."

Laura was lucky. She had all the things that Katie hadn't got and wanted so badly. She had caring parents, a lovely house and garden, and a beautiful golden spaniel puppy called Russet. She was generous and friendly, and everyone liked her.

Laura had told her mother all about Katie and Nick when they had arrived at the local school looking so unhappy. There were only two classes in the school, which was tiny, so Laura, Katie and Nick were in the same class, although Nick was going to the grammar school in the nearest town the following term. Their class had twenty-two pupils in it aged between seven and eleven, so the three children had become very close friends since February. Mrs Greyling sometimes asked Nick and Katie to tea and for a little while they were able to forget their loneliness.

The three of them walked home from school together most days and if Katie and Nick weren't expected back to do something for Aunt Margaret, they often went into Faldham Woods to play and to climb trees. If it rained, they went back to Laura's house and played games or listened to music.

"I like you and Nick best of everyone at school," Laura had said to them. "We like the same games and we laugh at the same things. I haven't any brothers or sisters, and I'm lonely sometimes. You're lucky to have each other."

"And you're lucky to have parents," Katie had answered at once. "Your mother is lovely. She hardly ever scolds, does she? And she's always so kind. You must love her a lot!"

"I do, and Dad too," Laura had said. "They like you, and they say you can come and play with me whenever you want to."

The children had told Laura about their Aunt Margaret, and had warned her of her bad temper. But Laura, coming from a loving family, couldn't imagine anyone like that.

However, after one or two undeserved scoldings Laura had decided to keep away from the bad-tempered woman, and now the children only met in the woods, or at Laura's house.

They were pleased to see her that afternoon, as she came through the trees to find them. She saw Katie's red eyes at once.

"What's the matter?" she asked, sitting down beside her. "Been getting into trouble with your aunt again? I do think she's horrible."

Nick told her their aunt had said that she didn't want them, and grudged every penny she had to spend on them. He also told her that she'd refused to give them the money they needed for the trip to the seaside.

"Well, that's easy," said Laura, jumping up. "I'm sure I've got more than enough in my money-box at home. I'll go and get it for you."

"No, Laura," said Nick. "We can't take your money. Thank you all the same. You're always so generous, but we just can't take it."

"Why not?" said Laura. "I shan't enjoy the school trip if you're not there. You're being silly."

"I would take it if I thought I could pay you back," said Nick. "But I know I can't."

"We couldn't take your money, Laura," said Katie, who, badly as she wanted to go on the trip, thought the same as Nick. "We could never, never pay it back."

"I don't want you to, idiot!" said Laura, beginning to look indignant.

"It's just that we don't like taking money for nothing, Laura," said Nick. "If we could do something in return for it, we would take it."

Laura thought for a moment. "I know what you could do!" she said, cheering up.

"You remember those lovely little baskets you brought to school, made from the rushes that grow by the stream? Well, will you make me some of those for the sale next week? I can fill them with raspberries from the garden and Mum can sell them. The money is to go towards building a new hospital in the next town so it's a good cause, isn't it? You would help Mum to make a lot of money if you let me buy the baskets."

Katie's eyes shone. This did seem a very good way out. She turned to Nick, who still looked a bit doubtful. "Nick! Let's make the baskets, and fill them with wild raspberries ourselves. We know where plenty grow. We'll charge Laura for the baskets, and her mother can sell them."

"All right," said Nick. "We'd be earning the money then, and I don't mind that."

"Good," said Laura. "I'll get the money now, and you can make the baskets in time for the sale, and fill them with wild raspberries the day before."

She sped off. Katie took Nick's arm and gave it a tight squeeze. She was overjoyed. She had so few treats now, and a day by the sea would be marvellous.

"Laura's quite something," said Nick. "We'll make some extra special baskets for her, Katie. We might as well make one or two now while we're waiting. Come on down to the stream."

They picked the long narrow leaves they needed for weaving the little baskets, and then sat down to work. Both children were clever with their fingers, and soon two neat baskets began to take shape.

Laura appeared again, rather out of breath. "Here you are," she said, and held out a handful of coins. "Now we can all enjoy tomorrow together. Oh, you've begun on the baskets already – aren't they pretty?"

"Thank you," said Nick, putting the money carefully into his pocket. He wondered whether or not to tell his aunt they were going on the school trip after all. He decided that he wouldn't. She might make him give up the money to her!

"We'll say nothing to Aunt Margaret about it," he said to Katie. "Save your supper tonight, if we get any, and we'll have it for our lunch tomorrow. I daren't ask Aunt Margaret for sandwiches in case she guesses we've got the money for the trip."

"I must go now," said Laura. "Mum wants me to do something with her. See you tomorrow and don't be late or the coach will go without you!"

"Goodbye, and thanks very much," said Nick. Katie walked with her a little way, then ran back to Nick, who was finishing off his basket very neatly with a strong handle.

"What fun! We're really going on the trip tomorrow!" said Katie, her brown eyes shining with joy. "Oh, Nick, I can't wait to see the sea again!"

"Yes," agreed Nick. "It seems a long time since last year!"

"Well, it was always such fun at Swanage," said Katie, "especially last year when we rescued Sophie and David and hid in that little temple on the island."

"That was a really good adventure," replied Nick. "I hope they're happy now and that whoever is looking after them is kind."

"I never imagined we'd be orphans like them six months later," said Katie. "I wish I knew their address, but they don't know where we live now and we don't know where their new home is."

"They know we lived next door to Mike and Penny, so maybe they could get our address through them," said Nick. "There, that basket is finished. I'll hide it under this thick bush. Bring yours here too."

He hid the two little baskets, and then they went back to the cottage. Aunt Margaret was sitting outside in the garden, mending. She did everything very fast, even sewing, and her needle seemed to fly in and out. She looked up as the children came along.

"There's some weeding to be done," she began, as soon as she saw them. "You'll just have time to do it before you go to bed. Do it well, or there'll be no supper for you."

"Yes, Aunt Margaret," said Katie meekly, thinking that she didn't mind how much weeding she did, now that she was sure of going on the school trip the next day. They set to work and not even their aunt could find fault with the way they weeded that onion bed!

"You'll find your supper in the fridge, on the blue plate," said Aunt Margaret, when they had finished. "Eat it, and go to bed."

Their uncle hadn't come back. He sometimes stayed away for hours, to be out of reach of his wife's sharp tongue. Nick and Katie went indoors and opened the fridge door. On a plate were two thick cheese sandwiches.

They were hungry, but they knew they must save the sandwiches for the picnic lunch. Keeping an eye on their aunt through the window, they took some paper and quickly wrapped up the two sandwiches. Nick stuffed them into his rucksack.

"We'll take a bottle of water too," he said, and filled an old lemonade bottle at the tap. He put it in with the sandwiches.

"Now let's go up to bed before Aunt begins to ask awkward questions!" said Nick. "Take care not to mention the trip at breakfast, Katie!"

Up to bed they went. Nick hid the money Laura had given him under his pillow. It was too precious even to leave in his jeans pocket! It meant a whole day by the sea for both of them.

CHAPTER 3

A Day by the Sea

Katie awoke feeling very excited. It was early, but she couldn't go to sleep again. She wished she had something new and smart to wear for the trip.

Aunt Margaret's voice came in through the door. "It's time to get up, Katie. Go down and lay the breakfast-table."

Nick helped Katie to lay the table, and both children looked in delight at the sunny day outside. "It's going to be fine," said Nick. "Isn't that good? The sea will be as blue as forget-me-nots."

"Shh! Here comes Aunt Margaret," whispered Katie. They had breakfast. Their uncle was lost in his newspaper, looking sulky. He glanced at the children, and wished he had some money to give them. He was fond of them, but he had to hand over all that he earned to Aunt Margaret.

Aunt Margaret made a few remarks to

him about going off to look for work as soon as breakfast was finished. He scowled at her.

"Nagging for breakfast, nagging for lunch, nagging for tea," he growled. "I tell you, one of these days you'll nag me out of this house!"

"It's a pity you don't go," said Aunt Margaret. "There'd be one mouth less to feed."

The children said nothing. It was always safer to keep quiet when Aunt Margaret was cross. They were longing to get away to school. Nick could feel the precious coins almost burning a hole in his pocket. Aunt Margaret didn't know about them, so she couldn't take them away.

But Katie, who dreaded her aunt's sharp, piercing eyes, thought she might be able to sense the money in Nick's pocket. She fidgeted, longing to leave the table and go.

"For goodness sake, Katie, what's the matter with you this morning?" said Aunt Margaret at last. "Stop fidgeting. Be off to school before I get really annoyed!"

Katie shot off at once, and pretended not to hear when her aunt shouted to her to come back and clear things away. Nick came out soon after, his schoolbag on his back and a broad grin on his face.

"Aunt can't make out why we're not moaning and groaning because we can't go on the school trip!" he said. "We ought to have looked sad and sorrowful. You nearly gave the game away, you looked so excited, Katie."

"I can't help it," said Katie, and skipped off beside Nick. "I feel so happy. A whole day's holiday by the sea! I can't wait to swim through the waves again. And we'll find some shells and seaweed."

Then a thought struck her, and she turned to Nick, looking scared. "What will Aunt Margaret say when we don't go home to lunch?"

"She'll guess where we are all right," said Nick. "She'll think Mrs Hall paid for us, I expect. We mustn't tell her we got the money from Laura."

"I hate not being honest with Aunt Margaret," said Katie. "Oh, Nick, I wish we needn't deceive her. We'd never have thought of deceiving Mum."

"We're not doing any harm," said Nick.

"We'll be earning the money ourselves by making the baskets. We're not robbing Aunt Margaret. Still, it would be nicer if we could trust her and tell her everything."

The whole school was in uproar. Every child was going on the trip. The coach pulled up outside the school playground and the excited children started to climb in.

As Nick and Katie waited to get on the coach, Aunt Margaret appeared, walking along the street on her way to the village shop where she worked. Katie saw her first and stared in horror. She pulled at Nick's arm.

"Quick! Hide behind Mrs Hall, or Aunt'll see us as she passes the school."

"No. Get into the coach before she spots us," Nick whispered.

They pushed forward and were just climbing in when their aunt did see them. She stared in surprise, and then looked most annoyed. Who had paid for them? Where had they got the money? She hurried down the road towards the coach as Mrs Hall got on with the last of the children.

"Oh, coach, do start. Hurry, please!"

cried Katie to herself, her heart beating fast. "Quick, before Aunt Margaret comes!"

Her aunt came up behind the coach just as it began to move. She called out loudly. "Nick! Katie!"

She ran after it, waving, but luckily no one realised that she was trying to stop the coach. In a moment Aunt Margaret was left behind and the children were safe.

"We're really off!" said Nick thankfully. "She can't catch us now, Katie."

Laura was sitting at the back of the coach with Nick and Katie.

"Gosh, I thought she was going to jump into the coach and pull you out by your ears," she said. "She looked dreadfully angry. What will she do to you when you get back home?"

"We won't think about it," said Nick. "We're going to enjoy every minute of freedom that we've got!"

It was a lovely day. The sea was as blue as the sky and edged with little waves that seemed to spill foamy white lace round their feet. The sun shone down and the water was cool to swim in.

All the children were hungry at lunch-time, especially Katie and Nick who had had no supper the night before. They gobbled up their two cheese sandwiches in no time. Laura sat beside them and unwrapped an enormous packet of sandwiches with hard-boiled eggs and tomatoes as well. She handed some to Nick and Katie.

"Mum guessed you wouldn't be able to bring much lunch, so she's given me extra of everything for you to share," she said. "There are crisps and chocolate and apples as well."

Nick and Katie ate everything hungrily. Laura had even brought extra cans of drink for them.

After lunch the two girls wandered off to hunt for shells and seaweed while Nick sat with his bird book open, watching the different seagulls. Katie found some lovely shells. She held a big whelk shell to her ear and dropped it hastily when she found a hermit crab living inside it.

The older children played French cricket and football on the sands and then cooled off in the sea again, while the little ones made sandcastles with moats and dug

channels for the incoming tide to fill up.

Tea was lovely, and there was plenty of it. Then, after a last hour of wandering along the edge of the waves, it was time to climb into the coach and go home.

Nick and Katie were very silent as the coach sped along. What would their aunt say to them?

"Let's tell her Mrs Hall paid for us," said Katie.

"That's a lie," said Nick. "We can't possibly say that."

"Say you earned the money yourselves," suggested Laura. "After all, that's quite true."

The nearer they got to Faldham the more the children worried. It was dreadful to be going home to someone they were so afraid of.

"I'll give Aunt Margaret some of my shells," said Katie. "Perhaps that will please her."

There were many mothers at school to meet their children. Katie looked round at them enviously. Mrs Greyling was there to meet Laura and she smiled at them.

"I'm sorry I can't give you a lift, but I've

got to take Laura to her piano lesson," she said.

"That's all right," said Nick. "We've had a wonderful time. And thank you for the smashing food you sent for us. We would have starved without it!"

Katie and Nick thanked their teacher for a lovely day, and then trailed miserably home. They walked more and more slowly as they came near to their aunt's cottage. They stood in the garden, hardly daring to go in.

The door flew open and Aunt Margaret stood there, her eyes angry and sharp, and her thin-lipped mouth set in a straight line.

"So you've come at last! And where did you get the money from to go on the trip, I'd like to know? You got it out of your uncle, didn't you? I've told him what I think of him, giving you money that he keeps from me! You bad children! Deceiving me, and making him deceive me too!"

"Uncle didn't give us any money," said Nick in surprise. "We did ask him, but he said he only had a few pence. Oh, I hope you didn't go on at him, Aunt, because he really didn't give us the money, so he didn't lie to you."

"Well, where did you get it from then?" cried his aunt. "You just tell me, before I go to your teacher and find out!"

"Please don't go and make a fuss at school," begged Katie. "We earned the money, Aunt Margaret. We earned it ourselves, we really did."

"You earned some money and didn't give it to me!" said her aunt, speaking as if she was immensely astonished. "When you know your uncle is out of work and I've hardly any money left! Ungrateful, mean children! I've a good mind to say I won't keep you a week more! I've a good mind to pack you off to a foster home somewhere and get rid of you. Go up to bed, before I really lose my temper."

The children ran upstairs, each getting a glare as they passed their angry aunt.

Katie whispered fearfully, "She won't really send us to a foster home, will she, Nick? She won't really get rid of us, will she? Oh, Nick, it was such a lovely day we had, and now it's all spoilt!"

"No, it isn't. We'll remember the yellow

sands and the blueness of the sea, and the feel of the water on our feet," said Nick. "Nothing can spoil that. Get into bed quickly, Katie, you look half asleep already!"

They were soon both in bed. Katie fell asleep almost at once, but Nick lay awake for some time. He heard his uncle come in. He heard his aunt's complaining voice and guessed she was telling his uncle about their ingratitude in daring to keep for themselves the money they had earned.

"We must remember to finish making all those baskets for Laura," thought Nick, closing his eyes. "I'll make some tomorrow. Oh, what a lovely day we've had!"

He fell asleep while his aunt's voice below went on and on and on. It seemed to change into the sound of the sea, and Nick dreamed peacefully of the waves breaking on the shore.

CHAPTER 4

THREE CHILDREN – AND RUSSET

Nick slipped into Katie's room very early the next morning. "Katie, listen! You'd better give Aunt Margaret the shells we brought back. If we don't try to put her in a good temper she'll scold all day long. It's Saturday, so we shan't be able to get away to school."

"All right," said Katie sleepily. She looked at the pretty shells on her chest of drawers. She didn't want to give them away at all.

Aunt Margaret was still in a bad temper. She was angry with the children for deceiving her, she was angry to think they had managed to get the money for the trip and wouldn't tell her where they had got it, and she was angry because she had accused Uncle Charlie of giving it to them when he hadn't. It put her in the wrong, and she didn't like that.

"Now," said Uncle Charlie, setting the newspaper up in front of him at the breakfast table. "Now, Margaret, just you hold your tongue this morning. The children have told you I didn't give them the money, so you wasted your breath yesterday telling me I did! Let's have a little peace."

"Aunt Margaret, here are some shells we brought back for you," said Katie hastily, and she put a handful of pretty little shells beside her aunt's plate.

"Do you think that shells can make up for being such mean, deceitful children?" said her aunt in a scornful voice. She got up from the table, taking the shells with her. To the children's dismay, she went to the kitchen and flung the shells into the rubbish bin!

"Oh, Aunt Margaret! I did like my shells," cried Katie angrily. "If you didn't want them, you could have let me keep them."

"Hold your tongue!" said her aunt, in the kind of voice that meant trouble would soon be coming. "I don't want to see either of you today. You can take your lunch and tea and get out. Don't come back till bedtime."

Nobody said anything more. Uncle Charlie read the paper, then folded it up and went out. The children washed up the breakfast things, and then hung around wondering if their aunt was going to give them their picnic for lunch and tea. She kept them waiting for a good while, and then cut some cheese sandwiches and some jam sandwiches.

She slapped them down on the table. "I hope you're ashamed of yourselves," she said. "I give you a home and look after you and you show no gratitude at all!"

"It's not much of a home!" said Katie, before she could stop herself. Nick gave her a sharp nudge. It was silly to say things like that to Aunt Margaret.

"One of these days I'll—" began Aunt Margaret fiercely. But the children fled, taking their sandwiches with them. They felt they couldn't bear to listen to another word.

They went to the wood and waited for Laura to come. Katie cried out in delight when she saw who was with her.

"You've brought Russet! Oh, Russet, I'm so pleased to see you!"

Russet was a puppy of seven months, a golden spaniel with melting brown eyes, drooping ears and a plumy tail. He belonged to Laura and she loved him with all her heart.

"I've brushed his silky coat today. Doesn't it shine beautifully?" said Laura proudly. "Russet, show them what you've just learned. Shake hands, now!"

Russet sat down and put up his left paw, cocking his head on one side in a very knowing way.

"Oh, no Russet, no," said Laura. "The other paw, please!"

Russet obligingly put up the other paw and Laura shook it. "How do you do?" she said.

"Woof, woof," answered Russet in a polite voice.

"Isn't he clever?" said Katie. "Russet, shake hands with me now!"

Russet did so, first with one paw and then the other.

Nick and Katie loved him nearly as much as Laura did. He wasn't as clever as their dog, Punch, was, but he was still only a puppy and had plenty of time to learn. He often played hide-and-seek with them, although he gave away Laura's hiding-place every time.

"Has he been naughty lately?" asked Katie, holding one of Russet's droopy ears in her hand.

"Yes, awfully," said Laura, looking rather sad. "I wish he wasn't. I know Mum won't keep him if he goes on being so bad."

"What's he done?" asked Nick.

"Well, he got on Mum's bed last night and chewed the top of her bedclothes to pieces," said Laura. "And this morning he somehow got a steak pie off the kitchen table and ate it all."

"Oh Russet, you're a silly dog," said Katie, looking into the spaniel's big brown eyes. "You look so very good. But you'll lose Laura and your lovely home if you go on being naughty."

"It's just mischief really," said Laura. "But he ought to be growing up now and being more sensible. You must learn to behave properly, Russet."

"Woof," agreed Russet, putting a paw

out, as if shaking hands would make things better.

"It doesn't matter if you chew my things," said Laura. "I'd never send you away, but it's serious when you damage other people's things. I'm sure if you steal things from the kitchen again you'll be shut up in your kennel. And you won't like that, you know."

"Woof," said Russet, looking solemn.

"He understands every word," said Nick, tickling Russet's sides. "Laura, we've got our lunch and tea with us. We haven't got to go back home at all today. Would your mum let you bring your lunch and tea out too, and we could explore the wood seriously? It stretches for miles and we could go quite a long way into it."

"We might get lost," said Katie. "We don't know more than this edge of it."

The children looked back into the wood. The trees seemed thick and dark behind them. People had been lost in there. Once Nick had gone exploring, and was lucky to have found the way back again.

Laura's eyes lit up in the way they always did when she had a good idea.

"I know! We'll go right into the heart of the woods today. We won't lose our way because we'll use the idea from the story Mrs Hall read us in class last term. You remember – where they tied string to a tree, and unravelled the ball as they walked into the wood. Then, when they wanted to find their way out, they only had to follow the string back again!"

"Oh yes! That would be a good idea!" said Nick, sitting up. "Go home and fetch some food and see if you can find an enormous ball of string as well."

Laura jumped up. "I'll go and ask Mum if I can have my lunch and tea in the woods with you, and I'll ask Dad if I can have some of his string. I know he keeps some big balls of it in the hall cupboard."

"Great!" said Katie. "While you're away we'll make a few more baskets, Laura. We mustn't forget we need to make twenty altogether."

"Leave Russet with us," said Nick. "He can look for rabbits."

But Russet wouldn't stay. Where Laura went he had to go too. He loved her as much as she loved him. So off the two went together, Russet close to Laura's flying heels.

"We'll get the rushes from the stream," said Nick, getting up. "Laura won't be back for an hour, I should think. We can make several baskets in that time. You've still got to make a handle for your first one, too, haven't you?"

Nick brought back some rushes, and the two set to work. Soon four little baskets, light yet strong, lay on the grass beside them. "When they're filled with wild raspberries they'll look great," said Nick. "It was a good idea of Laura's. There are plenty of raspberries deeper in the woods."

"It'll be exciting to go right into the heart of Faldham Woods," said Katie.

"Yes," said Nick, laughing. "Perhaps we shall be the first ones to reach it."

Katie felt a delicious shiver creep down her back. Woods were mysterious and anything might happen in their depths.

"I suppose we might discover the hideout of a gang of thieves," said Katie.

Nick shook his head. "I doubt it. There haven't been any burglaries reported near here recently."

"The woods stretch for miles, don't they?" said Katie. "Are there any paths that go all the way through?"

"No, there won't be proper paths further in – only rabbit runs," answered Nick. "But we'll have Russet with us, so you needn't worry."

"I'm not worried!" said Katie indignantly. "I just hope it won't turn into a tangle of brambles and bushes."

"I don't think so," said Nick, finishing off a basket. "This was once part of a forest and its centre will be full of tall trees pressing together with sunlight peeping through the canopy."

Almost an hour went by, and then they heard Laura's excited voice.

"Where are you? Oh, there you are! I've got my lunch and tea, and I've got the most enormous ball of string you ever saw! I've remembered to bring a bone for Russet, too. And I've got some lemonade for us all!"

"Oh good! Your mum is kind!" said Nick, pleased. "Mind my baskets, Russet. Take your big paws off that one! We're all ready to explore Faldham Woods now!"

CHAPTER 5

IN THE HEART OF THE WOOD

Panting slightly, Laura sat down and eased a bulging rucksack off her back.

"What have you brought?" said Nick, looking at it in astonishment.

"Oh, egg sandwiches, tomatoes and a bit of salt, jam tarts and cherry cake!" said Laura. "Enough for all of us. I know what your mean old aunt is like. She's probably given you stale bread and leftover cheese!"

This was quite true. Nick and Katie looked at Laura gratefully. She always tried to share everything with them. Nick took the bag from Laura.

"I'll carry this," he said. "Ugh, what's that smell?"

"Only Russet's bone," said Laura. "It's wrapped up in that bit of paper. He likes them smelly. If they aren't smelly enough he buries them till they are. He nearly got shut up in his kennel just before I came back. He misbehaved again."

"What did he do?" asked Katie.

"He found Mum's bedroom slippers and chewed the heel off one," said Laura. "Mum was awfully cross, because they were new ones."

Katie looked anxiously at Russet. "You really will have to turn over a new leaf," she said. "You'll be given away if you don't. You wouldn't like that, would you?"

"Woof," said Russet, and wagged his tail. He offered Katie a paw.

"He keeps wanting to shake hands with everyone now," said Laura. "He put his paw out to the cat, too, and she hissed at him."

"Come on, we'd better make a start," said Nick, laughing. "Wow! That certainly is an enormous ball of string, Laura! There must be miles of it. It's so thin and yet so strong. Just what we want."

"Now we tie the beginning of it to a tree, don't we?" said Laura. "Then we hold the ball as we walk into the wood and let the string unwind behind us. It'll be fun. We'll take turns at it."

They set off into the wood. They purposely left the path and wandered into the wilder parts, knowing that with the string to guide them safely back, they couldn't get lost.

"I don't expect anyone but rabbits has been here before," said Katie. "Let me have the ball of string now, Laura. I'd like to have a turn."

Laura gave it to Katie who marched along, letting the thin string unravel from the ball behind her. The trees grew closer together. Not so much sunlight came through. Sometimes the ground was bare beneath the trees, sometimes there was thin green grass. Leaves rustled softly when the breeze blew.

"It's getting mysterious," whispered Katie. "Here, Nick, you take the string now. It's your turn. We must have left miles of it behind us."

They walked for an hour or two, and then came to a little clearing. It was just a patch of grass where no trees grew. The sun shone down, gilding the grass and the children ran to it gladly.

"This is where we'll have our picnic," said Nick, throwing himself down in the warm sun, "I'm hungry now. Oh, Russet, don't lick my nose away! Katie, this must be almost the heart of the wood! What a brilliant place to find."

"It feels kind of magic," said Laura, and she sat down in the middle of the clearing. Katie flopped down beside her. Russet went to the bag and sniffed at it. He tried to paw out his bone.

"Wait, Russet," said Nick. "Let's get our breath back before we have lunch. Lie down and keep still for a minute."

But that was impossible for Russet. He wandered round, sniffing here and there, and then barked loudly. He wanted his bone. Nick groaned and reached for the bag. "You're a most impatient dog," he said. "Well, here you are. Wait till I take the paper off! Russet, *wait*!"

The sight of the things in the bag made Nick want his own lunch. So he handed out the packets to Laura and they all began to eat. Tomatoes dipped in salt were delicious, Katie thought. The cherry cake was lovely, too. Mrs Greyling had cut three very big slices. There were three bars of chocolate as well.

"Don't undo the sandwiches marked

with a T," said Laura. "We must keep those for this afternoon. There's some more cherry cake, I think."

"We'll have some lemonade now," said Nick, "and keep the rest for teatime. Russet, take your bone right away, please. It smells awful!"

Russet was enjoying his smelly bone. He chewed it and gnawed it, he sucked out bits of marrow and he licked every scrap of meat on it. It was a good bone. Russet made a fine meal of it and then wondered what to do with the rest.

"He's going to save up some for tea," said Katie, watching Russet wander off with his bone. "He's going to find some safe place to bury it. Isn't he funny?"

The three children lay down on their backs, and let the warm sun play on their faces and bare legs. They felt sleepy.

"Let's have a rest," said Nick.

Katie yawned, shutting her eyes tightly. "I'm really tired," she said. "It must have been the sea air yesterday."

"Where's Russet?" said Laura, sitting up and looking round. "Russet! Russet!"

A bark came from somewhere near.

Laura lay down again. "He'll come when he's finished burying that bone, I suppose. I only hope he won't wake us all up by licking our faces like he sometimes does."

It wasn't long before the children were asleep. They slept for about half an hour, then Laura woke with a jump. What had woken her? She sat up. The others were still asleep. Laura was about to lie down again when a doleful sound came to her ears.

It was Russet howling dismally! "Woooh! Woooo-ooooh!"

"Russet! What's the matter?" shouted Laura. The others woke up suddenly. Nick sat up at once.

"What's the matter?" he said to Laura, seeing her startled face.

"It's Russet. Listen!" said Laura. The whining and yelping began again, and Nick stood up.

"I hope he hasn't got caught in a trap," he said. "Come on! We must find him."

"The string, the string," shouted Katie, as they rushed to the edge of the clearing. "Let's get that, or we could lose ourselves. We might not be able to find our way back to this clearing!"

"Quite right," said Nick, and ran to pick up the ball of string, which was now very small indeed. They set off in the direction of Russet's whines.

"Woooo-ooooh! Woooo-ooooh!" cried Russet, sounding curiously muffled.

"Has he gone down a rabbit-hole and got stuck, do you think?" said Laura anxiously.

"Shouldn't think so," said Nick. "All I hope is he hasn't got his paw in a trap. Those traps are such cruel things. They cause the most dreadful injuries."

They set off in the direction of the howls. They went between the thick trees, and then stood still and listened.

"Over there," said Nick, as the howling began again. "Round this clump of trees."

They ran round the trees, and then all three stopped in amazement. In front of them was one of the biggest trees they had ever seen.

"It's an oak tree," said Nick. "An enormous old oak tree! It must be hundreds of years old, I should think. Look at its great trunk – twenty people could stand inside it, easily!"

"The howling is coming from inside that

tree, surely," said Laura, and she ran towards it.

As soon as she spoke, Russet set up a terrific whining again, and they heard the noise of scratching and jumping.

"He *is* in the tree!" cried Katie. "Russet, Russet, are you in there?"

"Woof, woof!" came a joyful bark. Now that he knew the children were near at hand, Russet felt sure he would soon be rescued. "Woooof!"

The children looked at the huge trunk. "It must be hollow inside," said Nick. "It sounds as if Russet's in the middle of it. No wonder his barks and yelps sounded so muffled. Russet, how did you get in?"

"Woof," said Russet, and scratched hard somewhere.

"Get out where you got in, silly," said Laura. But Russet didn't know where he had got in.

"We'll have to get him out somehow," said Nick. "But how on earth can we?"

CHAPTER 6

THE OLD HOLLOW TREE

"Let's walk all round the tree," said Katie. "Russet must have crept in at a hole to hide his bone."

They began to walk round the vast trunk. They found a small hole at last, at the bottom of the trunk. Nick poked a stick inside.

"Russet! Russet! See this stick! You must have got in at this hole, so you can get out by it. Come on, Russet!"

But for some reason Russet couldn't get out of the hole. He sat inside the tree and howled dismally again.

"Isn't he stupid?" said Laura, kneeling down by the hole. "Why can't he come out when we've shown him the way? Russet, don't be an idiot! Here, Russet! Here!"

Another long howl came from the tree. And idea struck Nick.

"Perhaps he's hurt himself or got stuck.

Perhaps we'd better climb up the tree and see if there's any way of getting down to rescue him."

They all looked up into the oak tree. It wouldn't be very difficult to climb. "I'll go," said Nick. "Give me a leg-up, Katie."

He was soon up on the big lowest branch. He climbed a little higher, and then looked down, trying to see if there was any way into the middle of the tree. It must be hollow if Russet had managed to squeeze in there!

But he could see no way in, so he climbed higher still, and gave a cry of surprise. He could look right down into the hollow trunk of the great tree! It had rotted away over many years, and now the old tree was nothing but a dying shell, still putting out leaves on its great boughs, but fewer and fewer each year.

"Katie! Laura! The whole of the tree is hollow! It's as big as a room. And the branches up here are so big and broad that I can lie on them easily without falling off!"

A howl came up to him. Russet wanted to be rescued and couldn't imagine why the children were so long about it.

"All right, Russet. I know how to reach you now," said Nick.

"Don't you get stuck inside the tree too!" called Laura anxiously. "Take care, Nick."

"You bet," answered Nick cheerfully. "Here I go – sliding down and down – right into the old hollow tree!"

The girls heard a thud and knew that Nick had landed on the ground inside. Then there came a collection of loud and joyful barks from Russet, who was evidently flinging himself on Nick in delight.

"What's it like in there?" called Katie, who was longing to explore the tree herself.

"Weird!" shouted back Nick, his voice sounding muffled. "It's so big we could fit a bed in easily. It's the most wonderful hiding place in the world! Get down, Russet, you idiot. Let me look round."

"Is it very dark?" yelled Laura.

"Very," said Nick. "But as far as I can make out, it's quite dry, and really spacious. Can you hear me knocking against the trunk?"

A sound like a woodpecker tapping on dead wood came to the ears of the listening girls.

"Yes! Of course we can hear you!" cried Laura. "We're coming up the tree, Nick, and we'll jump down too."

"Wait till I make sure I can get out all right," said Nick. He looked up, seeing the daylight above him, filtering through the branches of the great tree. He tried to swing himself up, but it was difficult.

"I think I can manage it," he said, "but we'll have to bring a rope if we're going to play inside the tree. Then we can fasten it to a branch above and haul ourselves up."

"Nick, can you see where Russet got in?" called Laura. "You'll never be able to get him out if you have to climb up yourself. You'll want both hands."

"Yes, I will," said Nick. "All right, I'll hunt around a bit, on my hands and knees. Oh, Russet, get off my back, I'm not playing tigers! Hey, there is some sort of hole. He must have gone in through that but a dead bough has fallen across it, so he can't squeeze out. I'll move it."

Nick dragged away the dead bough. He pushed Russet's nose to the hole. "Now you can get out, Russet. Go on, find the girls, quickly!"

Russet sniffed round the hole, and decided it was possible to wriggle through. To the girls' delight they saw his black nose appear, then his drooping ears, and finally his whole body, complete with wagging tail.

They patted him. "Were you playing a game of hide-and-seek, silly?" asked Katie. "You were lucky we found you!"

They went to the other side of the tree to watch Nick. He had managed to get out of the hollow trunk, and was climbing up higher. "There's a marvellous view over the

wood!" he called to the girls. "Come on up and see!"

Up they both climbed, leaving poor Russet whining below.

They sat about three-quarters of the way up the tree and looked out. The wind blew and the tree shook.

"It's like being on a ship," said Katie. "When the tree shakes in the wind, I can imagine I'm in a dinghy sailing across the bay and the tops of the green trees are like the open sea. It's a lovely feeling."

"We must be almost exactly in the middle of the wood," Laura said. "You can see the tree canopy stretching into the distance wherever you look. This great oak tree stands up high above all the others. I wonder how old it is."

"Look!" said Katie suddenly. "There's a hole in this branch here and a bigger hole still over there. Like little cupboards. We could hide things there."

"We could play here, and make ourselves a tree-house," said Laura, her eyes gleaming. "It's quite big enough to live in. The summer holidays will begin next week and we'll be able to meet every day. We could clean it out and turn it into our own secret place."

"Oh, yes. Nobody would know about it except us!" said Katie, who loved secrets. "We wouldn't tell anyone. It would be our own house and we could furnish it. I've got an old rug I could bring and Nick's got a stool he made himself. We could have a box for a table."

"I've got lots of things I could bring!" cried Laura. "We could take some of the furniture from the playhouse in the garden and put it inside the tree to make a proper house. Wouldn't it be fun!"

"We could use the rug as a carpet. And Katie, you've got an old dolls' tea set, haven't you?" said Nick, getting excited too. "We could have that for meals."

"No, that would be too small," said Laura, who knew the little tea set quite well. "I'll bring some old plates and mugs we used to take on picnics."

"We could keep some of the things in these holes in the branches," said Katie, putting her hand into one. "I suppose the owls have used them for their nests. They'd make good cupboards."

"That branch down there, the very broad one, would make a fine couch where it forks from the trunk," said Nick. "We could put a rug over it and lie there reading."

"The front door is through the middle of the tree," said Katie, "and the back door is the hole that Russet uses."

Everyone laughed. Russet, down below, gave a whine. He didn't like being left out of things like this.

"What about a lamp? It's dark down there," said Nick.

"Candles, of course!" said the two girls together. And Laura added, "Just think of sitting down in our tree-house by the light of candles! Nobody would guess where we were. It's the most exciting thing we've ever thought of!"

"Let's have our tea sitting on this broad branch, shall we?" said Nick. "It's great up here. I'll go down and get the food."

"Tell Russet to find his bone and have his tea, too," called Laura, laughing.

Russet was most indignant when Nick fetched the tea, addressed a few loving words to him, and then disappeared up the tree once more, leaving him behind. He whined loudly and scratched on the tree-trunk vigorously with his front paws. But it was impossible to carry him up.

The children divided the jam sandwiches and cake. They stood the lemonade cans in one of the cupboards. It was nice to see them there.

"We shall be able to make plans all this week and next, till the holidays begin," said Nick. "We'll collect everything we can for our tree-house. I've thought of lots of things already. My old clock, for instance. It would make it seem really like a house if we hear it ticking away down there."

"Good idea," said Katie. "We could bring a few books too."

"I'll bring some biscuits in a tin and some sweets in a jar," said Laura. "We'll always be glad of something extra to eat."

They talked until it was time to go back. Then down the tree they went to find the string that would lead them safely out of the wood. Russet was overjoyed to have them on the ground with him once more.

"Down, Russet, down!" said Laura. "Home we go! Where's the string? Here it is. I'd never find my way home without it!"

CHAPTER 7

EXCITING PLANS

Before they set off home, Nick tied the string firmly to a small tree at the edge of the little clearing. Now the end couldn't slip away, and they would be able to find the way back to the hollow tree whenever they wanted to. Taking hold of the thin brown string that ran twisting through the trees, Nick led the way home.

They would never have found the way back without help of this kind. There was no path to follow, nothing to guide them at all. It was evening now, and the sun lay low in the west. Nick ran his hand along the string and followed it through the darkening wood.

The girls didn't bother to touch the string. They followed Nick, and Russet ran here and there, sniffing at rabbit-holes, but never getting very far behind.

"I'm a bit tired of running my hand

along the string," said Nick at last. "Katie, you have a turn."

So Katie let herself be guided by the string and on they all went. Once Katie saw a flower she didn't know and left the string to look at it, then, when she looked for the string again, she couldn't find it!

"Oh no! Where is it?" she cried. "I'm sure it went round this tree!"

But it didn't. In a panic the other two searched for the string too, but it was very difficult to find in the fading light. They looked at one another in fright.

"Now what are we going to do?" said Nick. "Katie, you are an idiot, really! You might have had more sense than to let go of the string. It's a dreadfully difficult thing to see once you've lost it."

"I know. I'm awfully sorry," said poor Katie, almost in tears. "I just didn't think."

They hunted about a little more, but it was Russet who really found it. He was sniffing about for rabbits and suddenly got one leg caught in the string which, just there, had fallen rather low. He tugged, and set the whole bush in motion, as the string pulled against it.

"There it is, round Russet's leg. Look!" yelled Laura. "Oh Russet, what a clever dog you are!"

"Woof," said Russet modestly, and held out a paw. Everyone shook hands with him. They thought he deserved it.

Nick took the string himself. He felt that it was safest with him! Off they went again, and at last came into the part of the wood they knew. They said goodbye there.

"It's been a brilliant day," said Laura. "I shall think about it in bed tonight. It will be a lovely thing to go to sleep on!"

"Goodbye, Russet. Be good," said Katie, patting him. "Look, Laura, he knows he must shake hands when he says goodbye. He's putting out his paw so politely, only it's the wrong one again!"

Laura ran home, and Nick and Katie made their way back to their aunt's cottage. It was fun to have such an exciting secret, shared by the three of them and Russet. .

"You're late enough!" said Aunt Margaret when they got in. "There's no supper for you tonight, unless you want bread and cheese."

But the two children had feasted well on

Laura's food and were not hungry. They said goodnight and went up to bed, secretly glad that they were late and didn't need to sit up with their aunt.

Katie tried to keep awake to think about the tree-house. She imagined she was there, cosily inside, with a little candle flickering beside her. She imagined the trees in the wood outside, whispering together, while she sat in the oak tree, listening. Nobody would know where she was. How lovely it would be to have a place like that all for themselves!

The days went swiftly by and the end of term came. Aunt Margaret hated the holidays.

"Holidays again!" she said on Thursday, when they came home early, laden with their term's books. "It always seems to be holidays. Now I suppose that when I'm not at work I'll have you on top of me all day long! What with your uncle always at home too, I do have a time!"

"We'll try not to be a nuisance," said Nick cheerfully. "We'll go off to the woods and play every day, after we've done any jobs you want us to do."

"Yes, I'm the only one in this house that does any work!" grumbled their aunt. "Your uncle's out of work, and you play all day."

The children said nothing. Aunt Margaret was never satisfied with anything anyone did. There was no pleasing her!

The children looked about for things they could take to the tree-house: the old rug and a few ragged sacks; the little stool Nick had made at school and his clock; an old saucepan with half the handle gone and the bit of old candle left on a shelf in the shed.

"Nothing very much, but it will all help," said Nick.

"Anyway, Laura will be able to bring a nice lot of things," said Katie. "She's got plenty."

"Yes. But we must do our share too," said Nick. "We can't bring much, but we must take what we can. I shan't feel as if it's our house if we don't take something towards it too."

"I'm going to take my picture," said Katie suddenly. "The one that hangs over my bed-head."

"What – the one of Swanage Bay?" asked

Nick. "You can't! Aunt would miss it."

"It doesn't matter. It's mine," said Katie. "Mum gave it to me last Christmas. You know she did. Uncle Bob had to store so many things for us because there wasn't room to keep them here, but this reminds me of our holidays with Mum and Dad and I couldn't bear not to bring it with me."

"Of course it's yours," said Nick. "But if you take it away, Aunt Margaret is sure to ask where it's gone."

"I'm taking it," said Katie obstinately. "I want it in our tree-house. It's my favourite picture, and it would look lovely hanging on the trunk-wall of our house. I'll take a nail to hang it on and I'll use the heel of my shoe as a hammer."

She was pleased when she thought of her picture hanging on the wall of the tree-house, shining in the light of the candle there. It would make it feel like home.

The children gathered together their few things and hid them at the back of the old shed. Aunt Margaret was always poking about, and they didn't want her to find the things and ask questions. She must never know about the tree-house!

"I shan't take the picture off the wall till tomorrow," said Katie. "Not that Aunt Margaret will see it's gone! I do my own bedroom, and except for poking her nose in to check it's been done properly, she never comes in."

"I wonder what Laura will bring," said Nick. "She always has such good ideas. I hope she'll bring some matches. I daren't ask Aunt Margaret for any and we can't light the candle without matches."

They went off to bed feeling excited. They were to meet Laura at ten o'clock in the usual place in the wood. They hadn't seen her after they broke up, because it was her mother's charity sale and Laura had been helping. They had given her the twenty rush baskets filled with delicious wild raspberries. Laura had been very pleased.

"Mum will love them! You are clever! We shall make a lot of money out of them."

Friday morning came at last. The children did everything their aunt set them to do, keeping their eyes on the clock. At last it was time to go. They rushed to the shed to get their things, and Katie ran upstairs to fetch her picture.

"Now, off to the tree-house again!" said Nick, stuffing everything into an old sack. "We'll have a good time there today, Katie, won't we!"

CHAPTER 8

MOVING-IN DAY

Laura was waiting for them in their usual meeting place, looking very excited. She had an overflowing rucksack on her back and carried two enormous baskets.

"Wow, Laura, what have you brought with you?" exclaimed Katie. "And what's Russet got on his back?"

Russet was not looking very happy. He didn't come to greet the children as usual. He stood quite still with his tail drooping behind him. He had a package tied on his back.

"I thought Russet ought to help as well by carrying his own luggage," said Laura, laughing. "I've packed up some biscuits for him, and a ball, and wrapped them in one of his own little rugs. I tied them on his back for him to carry. But you don't like it, do you, Russet?"

Russet whined, and stood looking up at

the three children pleadingly, from soft brown eyes.

"It's not at all heavy, really," said Laura, looking at the package, "but when he runs it sort of slips sideways and hangs under his tummy, and he hates that."

"Between you, you've certainly brought a lot!" said Nick, pleased.

"I've brought my musical box that plays six different tunes when you wind it up," said Laura. "I thought it would sound lovely when we're sitting inside the tree. I expect you think it's a silly thing to bring, but I couldn't help wanting it."

The others didn't think it was silly. They thought it was a lovely idea. "I brought my clock," said Nick, "and Katie brought her picture. I hope Aunt Margaret doesn't miss them."

"Won't we have fun arranging everything?" cried Laura, picking up her two baskets. "Nick, you'll have to follow the string, because I haven't a single hand to use!"

"Give me one of the baskets," said Nick. "And if you like to take that enormous rucksack off your back, I'll carry that, too.

You can take my bundle. It's not nearly so heavy."

"Oh no, thanks," said Laura. "I like carrying it. But can you take one of the baskets? That would be a help. Now, Russet, are you ready? Come on, then. Look a bit more cheerful, do! And remember, you're still in disgrace!"

"Why, what's he done now?" asked Katie.

"He got into the hen-run and chased all the hens," said Laura. "He must have squeezed through under the wire. Daddy was very angry. I can't think why Russet doesn't develop a bit of sense. He must know he'll get into trouble if he chases hens. I've told him so heaps of times."

Russet trotted along sedately, cocking one eye up at Laura as she spoke his name. He knew he was still in disgrace. His package suddenly slipped off his back, slid round and hung under his tummy. He stopped and gave a howl.

"Katie, put it right for him, will you?" said Laura. "You can't tie it too tightly because it hurts him."

The three children went very slowly

through the wood, for they were all heavily laden. But it didn't matter. They were excited and happy. They had a tree-house to go to which they were going to furnish and make their own!

"This is our moving-in day!" said Katie happily, and that made the others laugh. "Well, it is! We're moving into our new home. Tree-House, Heart of the Wood. That's our new address."

"It would be funny if a postman delivered a letter to us at that address," said Laura.

Nick was following the string carefully. At last they came to the clearing where they had picnicked before.

"I thought we'd never get here," said Laura. "My back is just about breaking. What about having a rest and something to eat before we do any moving in?"

This seemed a very good idea to everyone, Russet as well. Nick untied the package from his back, and Russet at once rolled over on to his back and rubbed it against the ground. Then he sat down, hung out his long pink tongue and panted.

"You're not so out of breath as all that!"

said Laura, taking off her heavy rucksack. "You'd better go and find the bone you left behind yesterday. But if you get stuck in the tree again you can just stay there!"

It wasn't lunch-time yet. The children ate a bun each, and then decided to wait for another hour before they had a proper meal. They picked up their things, followed the string between the trees a little way further and came again to the enormous old oak tree. They stood still and looked at it.

"Come on, we can't stand here all day," said Nick at last. "There's plenty to do! First of all we'll climb the tree and haul everything up."

"We ought to have brought a rope!" said Laura. "I forgot about that!"

"I didn't," said Nick, and he undid a rope from round his waist. "I've got a good strong one. First we'll use it to haul up all our things one by one, and then we'll use it to lower ourselves down into the tree. I'll go up and tie one end to a branch."

Up he went, and took the rope with him. He tied one end firmly to a branch, and let down the other end. "Tie the biggest package on the end," he called. "Be sure you make a proper knot that won't slip, Katie."

Katie tied a firm knot. "Ready!" she called, and Nick hauled on the rope. Up went the big package, swinging between the branches. Nick pulled it on to the broad branch, settled it there firmly, and then let down the rope again.

Up came all the different bundles, until none was left. Laura and Katie climbed the tree, leaving Russet whining below and scraping at the trunk, trying to climb up himself.

Nick had everything on the broad branch. They peered down into the mysterious, hollow heart of the old tree. "You go down first, Nick," said Katie, "and we'll lower everything down to you. Then we'll both join you, and we'll light a candle and arrange all our belongings."

It was very exciting. The children felt happy as they worked. Nick slid down the rope into the hollow trunk and called up to the girls.

"I'm ready! Swing down the first lot on the rope. Not too quickly or you'll have it on my head."

Down came the bundles, one after another, and Nick caught them deftly as they entered the hole in the trunk. He put them on one side, and then called up again.

"Now you come on down. The rope will help you. Hang on to it, feel about with your feet, and let yourself slide down where you can. It's quite easy."

Laura came first, hanging on to the rope, slithering down into the hollow of the tree. She stood beside Nick, excited. Then came Katie.

"We're in our tree-house for the first time! Nick, light a candle!" she said.

"I haven't any matches," said Nick. "Did you bring any, Laura?"

Laura had brought two boxes, and a whole bunch of big candles! Nick was pleased. "We shan't want my little broken bit of candle after all," he said. "Which bundle are your candles in, Laura?"

"In the big basket," said Laura, and felt about for it. "Ah – here it is – and here's the bundle of candles – and the matches, too."

Nick pulled a candle from the bundle and lit it. A little flame flickered, then flared up. Nick held the candle high and

the three looked round their tree-house.

It was very big, nearly circular, and the walls were brown and rough. The ground they were standing on was quite dry. The tree didn't smell musty at all, which was lucky. About a metre above their heads was the hole down which they had come. The daylight, filtering dimly through the leaves above, had a greenish tinge.

"It's exciting, isn't it?" said Katie, taking a deep breath and looking around. "There's plenty of room for us all and here's Russet coming in at the back door!"

Sure enough, there was Russet, squeezing in at the small hole in the bottom of the trunk. He came panting in, thrilled to find the children there. He licked them and then sniffed solemnly round.

"What a secret to have!" said Laura. "Here we are, hidden away, and no one knows where we are!"

The candle flickered, and the shadows jumped round the hollow trunk. "Let's begin to arrange everything now," said Katie. "I'm longing to make this tree-room look like home. We'll undo the bundles first."

So they began. Moving into a tree-house was great fun. The three children hadn't been so happy for a long time!

CHAPTER 9

A LOVELY TREE-HOUSE

They found a little woody shelf sticking out
from one side of the tree-trunk, and they
decided to make it their mantelpiece. Laura
had brought a wooden candlestick and put
the candle into it, and balanced it carefully
on the rough shelf.

"Now let's unpack," said Laura. They set
to work to undo their packages, and soon
the floor was strewn with all kinds of
things.

The picture went up on the wall. Katie
hammered the nail into the wood with the
heel of her shoe, and then proudly hung the
picture there. The candlelight flickered on
it and the waves seemed to move. Nick
wound up his clock and put it on the
mantelpiece. *Tick-tock*, *tick-tock*, it went, and
the three children listened in delight.

"It seems to have got a much louder tick
inside this tree than it ever had at home,"

said Nick. "It's really a little alarm clock and we could set it if we needed to leave at a special time."

A bundle of rugs and cushions was placed at one side of the tree. "Just to sit on," said Laura. "We don't want beds, because we won't sleep here, worse luck!"

"Oh, wouldn't it be exciting if we did sleep here!" said Katie.

"It would be brilliant!" agreed Laura.

"Here's my old rug," said Nick, spreading it out. "It's rather holey, but fairly thick. Let's use it for carpet, shall we? The floor of the tree is a bit messy with twigs and dead leaves and things."

So the carpet was laid over the floor of the tree and it fitted well. Nick set his stool down at one side. "I think we'd better use the stool as a table till we get a box or something," he said. "We can sit on the floor, and put anything we want to on the stool."

"Here's my little musical box," said Laura, and put it on the mantelpiece beside the clock. "There's just room for it. Oh look, there's a hole in the wall of the tree here that would make an excellent cupboard. I'll put the candles and matches in there."

"They just fit! Doesn't it all look good?" said Katie joyfully. "We can put things in the two cupboards upstairs in the tree as well. You remember the holes we found."

"This is a most convenient tree," said Nick. "Great, Laura. You've brought a lovely lot of crockery: mugs, plates and a teapot and a jug. Here's a kettle, too. We can't boil water inside this tree, though, we might set it on fire."

"No," said Katie, "but we might want to boil a kettle outside in the wood, and then make tea for ourselves."

"Here's a tin of biscuits, a jar of sweets and box of chocolate," said Laura, unpacking them. "Not to eat now, to store away so that we shall always be able to have a meal if we want one. And here are three bottles of lemonade."

"You think of everything!" said Nick in admiration. "Great, you've even brought books to read!"

"And cards and some board games!" said Laura. "You see, it might rain sometimes when we're here, so we'll want something to do inside."

At last everything was unpacked and arranged. The children stared around their tree-house, really excited. It looked like a small, rather dark room, crowded with all their possessions. The clock ticked loudly, and the candle flickered over the rough brown walls.

"Now we'll have our lunch," said Laura happily. "Our first meal in our tree-house home!"

"It's a bit hot in here," said Nick. "Don't you think it would be better to have it outside, Laura?"

"Oh no!" cried the two girls at once. "We must have our first meal indoors, Nick!"

Russet squeezed in at the hole, having gone out to find the bone he had left behind the week before. He set the bone down on the carpet and wagged his tail.

"Pooh! It's smellier now," said Katie. "I think Russet had better have his lunch outside, don't you, Laura?"

So Russet was pushed out, but he came back in again at once, bringing the bone with him.

"It's no good, he'll keep on coming in," said Laura. "Let's undo our lunch and have it now, shall we? I'm awfully hungry."

They undid the food and had a lovely lunch. It certainly was hot inside the tree, but it was such fun that nobody really minded. They ate sandwiches and cake hungrily, and drank lemonade. They used the little stool as a table, and sat on cushions and rugs. The clock ticked away merrily.

"The tree must be very old, to have rotted away like this," said Nick. "It's only a shell, really. It's surprising that it can put out any leaves at all! Russet, you hurry up and finish that smelly bone. And don't bury it any more."

Russet took his bone outside and came back without it. Evidently he had buried it! Anyway, the tree-house smelled nicer without it. Russet cuddled up to Laura and she hugged him.

"Nicest dog in the world!" she said. "I don't know what I should do without you, I really don't!"

"Does he still sleep on your bed?" asked Nick.

Laura nodded. "He's not supposed to. He has an old rug on my windowsill and he's supposed to sleep there, but when he hears Mum and Dad go into their bedroom, he jumps off and leaps up on to my feet. He likes to cuddle into the bend of my knees if he can."

"Punch used to sleep like that," said Katie. "He slept with Nick to start with and then crept into my room in the early morning. If you ever get tired of Russet, Laura, we'll look after him."

"I shall never, never get tired of him," said Laura at once. "Nobody knows how much I love him."

"Woof," said Russet, laying his head on her knee.

"He understands," said Nick, patting him. "I think he's a lovely dog, even if he is awfully naughty. I love his silky soft coat and lovely droopy ears, and soft brown eyes. I wonder what he thinks of our tree-house."

"He probably thinks we've come to live in a kind of big wooden kennel!" said Katie, with a giggle.

"Everybody finished?" said Nick. "Well, let's go up into the tree and get a breath of fresh air, shall we? We could take up a rug or two and spread them on that enormously broad branch, and lie there."

They went up one by one, helping themselves by hauling on the rope. Nick took a couple of rugs on his shoulders.

They climbed to the big broad branch and, just where it joined the main trunk, they spread their two rugs. Then they settled down on them to rest.

It was lovely there. It had been a bit stuffy inside the hollow tree, but up here it was fresh and breezy, though the wind was warm. They liked the way the branch swayed about. It really did feel like a boat at sea.

Laura closed her eyes and fell asleep. So did Katie. Nick lay awake, looking up through the green leaves, glimpsing bits of blue sky between them as they moved.

They had tea up in the boughs of the old tree. Nick went down into the hollow to fetch their tomato sandwiches.

"We'd left the candle burning," he said. "I blew it out. The room inside the tree looked really exciting when I slipped down the rope into it. You'd have liked it!"

"We're very lucky," said Laura. "It's a most wonderful secret."

"Yes. I don't feel as if I shall mind a bit when Aunt Margaret scolds us," said Katie. "I shall just think of our beautiful tree-house, and she can scold all she likes!"

After a bit they climbed down the tree and played games in the clearing until Laura at last looked at her watch. "Bother! It's really time for me to go," she said.

They ran back to the oak tree to check that everything was tidy there.

"We'll come back tomorrow. Goodbye, little tree-house," said Katie, remembering to blow out the candle this time.

Then off they all went through the wood, following the string. What a wonderful day they'd had!

CHAPTER 10

TROUBLE WITH AUNT MARGARET

Nick and Katie found their aunt and uncle out when they got home. They were glad. Now they wouldn't have to answer any awkward questions about what they had been doing, and where they had been.

They took books and read quietly till their bedtime. Then they looked in the fridge. Yes, on the blue plate were some sandwiches for their supper. They ate them and went up to bed feeling quite tired.

"I shall lie and think about our tree-house, and how lovely it looks in the candlelight," said Katie. "Nick, there's one thing it hasn't got, that all houses have."

"What?" said Nick.

"A little window," said Katie. "Do you think we could possibly make one?"

"Well, the walls of the tree are very thick and solid," said Nick doubtfully. "I don't think we could, Katie."

"That part where Russet goes in and out is awfully crumbly," said Katie. "We might perhaps find a crumbly bit in the walls that we could scrape away to make a small window. It wouldn't matter how tiny it was. Then we could look out of it when we wanted to, and see what was going on in the wood."

"It would be great if we could," Nick agreed.

"I could hang a little curtain over it," said Katie dreamily. "Do you think we could put a pane of glass in, Nick?"

"Hey, wait till we make a window!" said Nick. "As a matter of fact, a hole would be a good idea, it would let a little fresh air in. We wouldn't want glass there at all. That's the only fault I have to find with the room inside the tree: it's stuffy when we're all in there with the candle burning."

"If we had a window to let in the daylight we wouldn't use the candle so much," said Katie. "Oh, I wish Laura was here so that we would talk to her about it. I'm sure she'd like a window too. Imagine peeping out into the wood through it!"

"Other people might see us then," said

Nick. "We'd have to make an outside curtain of moss or leaves, so that we could draw it down over the window if ever anyone came that way. We must never, never let anyone know of our secret."

Katie lay and thought about a mossy curtain for a long time. Then she heard the sound of footsteps down below, and their aunt's scolding voice filled the little cottage. Clearly Uncle Charlie was in trouble again.

The children couldn't help hearing everything. It was obvious that Uncle Charlie had been after a job, with Aunt Margaret at his elbow to make sure he got it, but it was equally clear that it was not a job he liked, because it meant getting up too early in the morning.

"I could have had a later shift," he kept saying. "I'll have to leave here at half past five to get to the garage on time. If I'd had the later shift they offered me I could have started at half past eight."

"Well, the early shift means more money, doesn't it?" said Aunt Margaret. "We've been short so long that you might as well make up for it now and bring in as much money as you can. You'll start out at half past five each day, on time, and keep that job, if I have to drag you there!"

Katie stuffed her fingers in her ears and thought again of her tree-house. Why did Aunt Margaret always scold so much? Nagging just made people feel really cross.

She fell asleep and dreamed of the tree-house and the little musical box playing its tinkling tunes.

Next morning there was a great clatter in the house at five o'clock. It was Aunt Margaret getting up to see that Uncle Charlie had his breakfast and set off for his new job in time. Again the scolding voice came up the stairs.

"If I hadn't woken up you'd have overslept as usual. Why didn't you set the alarm? I told you to."

"It's broken, I think," said Uncle Charlie, stuffing bread and marmalade into his mouth. "The bell won't ring."

Aunt Margaret fiddled with the clock, but the alarm wouldn't sound. Nick, lying comfortably in bed, listening to the talk downstairs, had a sudden shock.

"Well, never mind!" he heard his aunt say. "There's a little alarm clock in Nick's room. I'll set that tomorrow morning."

"Oh, no," thought Nick. "I'll have to fetch that clock today somehow. I hope I can get it back before Aunt sees it's gone. What bad luck that she should want it just now!"

He made up his mind to go off to the tree-house immediately after breakfast to retrieve the clock. But he couldn't because Aunt Margaret told the two children to weed the potato bed for her.

"Couldn't we do it tomorrow?" begged Nick. "Oh, no, tomorrow's Sunday. Well, Monday, then."

"That's right. Try to put off doing a job of work, just like your uncle!" said Aunt Margaret grimly. "You'll do as you're told, and weed that whole bed today. I want it hoed as well and all the rubbish collected up."

There was nothing for it but to do what they were told. There was no chance even to tell Laura to get the clock. Nick told Katie in a low voice, and the little girl looked worried.

"Oh dear. If Aunt misses your clock, she may go into my bedroom to see if anything is missing there. Oh, Nick, we mustn't tell her we've taken them to the tree-house."

"Of course not," said Nick. "That's absolutely secret."

They set to work to weed the potatoes. They did it thoroughly, but the ground was hard and it took a long time.

Nothing was said about the clock all morning. The children breathed sighs of relief when they went in to their lunch, and saw that Aunt Margaret looked fairly amiable.

There was a nice lunch too, and the children enjoyed it. It was clear that now Uncle Charlie had a job again, things would be better all round. How they hoped he would keep it!

They washed up the lunch things, wondering if their aunt would let them go off for the afternoon now.

"Can we have the afternoon to play, as we worked all morning?" asked Nick at last.

"Yes," said Aunt Margaret, "but be back by teatime. I shall want you to fetch something from the village for me then."

The children got up to go, very thankfully. Then they got a shock.

"Oh, before you go, run upstairs, Nick, and bring me down the alarm clock in your room," said his aunt. "Uncle's is broken, so we'll have to use yours. Go and get it."

Nick simply didn't know what to do or say. He stared at his aunt and she rapped impatiently on the table.

"Well, don't stand there staring at me! Go up and get it! Anyone would think you didn't know what a clock was!"

Nick turned and went upstairs with Katie. They stood in his bedroom, looking desperately at one another.

"What shall we say?" whispered Nick. "Quick! What shall we say?"

"Say it isn't here," said Katie. "That's quite true. It isn't here."

There didn't seem anything else to say. Their aunt's voice came sharply up the stairs.

"What are you doing? Bring the clock down at once!"

"It isn't here!" called Nick.

There was silence. "But it must be there!" cried his aunt. "I saw it only a few days ago. Use your eyes. It's on the chest of drawers."

"But it isn't, Aunt Margaret!" shouted Katie. "It really isn't."

Their aunt came running impatiently up the stairs. She glanced at the chest. The clock certainly wasn't there. She stared around the room. There was no clock to be seen anywhere.

"Well, it was there," she said. "I suppose your uncle's put it into our room. I'll see."

She went to look, but the clock wasn't there either, of course. She came out, puzzled.

"What's happened to it?" she said. She suddenly swung round on Nick and made him jump. "Have you broken it and hidden it away? Now, tell me the truth."

"No, Aunt Margaret, I haven't broken it," said Nick honestly.

"Nor have I," said Katie. "We would have told you if we had."

Feeling more and more puzzled, she went into Nick's room again and looked in the cupboard there. No clock! The children watched her, full of dismay. This was dreadful! Why did their uncle's clock have to go wrong just now?

"It may be in your room, Katie," said

Aunt Margaret, and went in there. Katie stared in horror. Now maybe her aunt would notice that the picture was gone! Aunt Margaret looked all round the room. No clock anywhere. Then she gazed at the wall over the bed, and a puzzled look came over her face. She frowned.

"There's something missing," she said. "Yes, that picture! Whatever has happened to the picture?"

CHAPTER 11

In Disgrace

The children stared in silence at their astonished aunt. They couldn't think of a word to say.

"Well! Have you lost your tongues?" she asked sharply. "Didn't you hear what I said? Where's the picture? Has that got broken too?"

"No," said Katie. "It's not broken any more than the clock is, Aunt Margaret."

"Then where is it?" said Aunt Margaret. The children looked at her in despair. They couldn't possibly tell her about the tree-house.

Aunt Margaret lost her temper. She caught hold of Katie and shook her hard. The little girl gasped. Nick tried to stop his aunt, and she pushed him away roughly.

"Now you just tell where those things are!" she said. "If you don't tell me at once, you'll go to bed for the rest of the day!

Taking my things like this and not letting me know!"

"We wouldn't have taken them if they'd been yours," said Nick. "The clock is mine. It belonged to my mother. And the picture was Katie's. We brought them with us when we came here. They're ours, not yours."

This speech made Aunt Margaret even more angry.

"So you *have* taken the things! Where are they? How dare you take things out of the house?"

"Aunt Margaret, we only took them because they were ours," said Nick.

"I know what you've done with them!" said Aunt Margaret, a sudden thought striking her. "You've sold them! That's how you got the money for going to the seaside, wasn't it? I might have guessed it was something like that. You bad, deceitful children."

"We didn't get our money through selling the picture and the clock," said Nick. "We only took them yesterday."

"Where did you take them?" demanded his aunt. The children wouldn't say. They stared at her, speechless. She pushed Katie into her room, and Nick into his, and slammed the doors shut.

"Now you can just stay in your bedrooms till you tell me where you've taken those things!" she cried and locked the doors. They heard her footsteps going downstairs, sounding sharp and angry.

Nick went to his door and put his mouth to the lock. "Katie! I'm glad you didn't give away our secret. I thought you might be afraid and tell."

"I was afraid, but I wasn't going to tell," said Katie, with tears in her voice. "Nick, isn't she unkind? Surely it isn't wrong to take our own things?"

"No, it isn't," said Nick. "Oh dear, I wonder how long Aunt will keep us here! If only she'd let us out we could go and get back the picture and the clock, and give them to her."

Their aunt came up at teatime. She unlocked Nick's door and came in. "Well?" she said. "Are you ready to tell me where the picture and the clock are?"

"I'll bring them back if you'll let me go and get them, Aunt Margaret," said poor Nick.

"I want to know where you've hidden them, and why," said his aunt. "I still believe you've sold them."

"Well, I haven't," said Nick. "And they're not exactly hidden either. We just wanted them for something, that's all. We can bring them back at once."

"I want to know where you've put them," said his aunt obstinately. She was really puzzled and bewildered as to why the children had taken such strange things away, and where they had put them. She couldn't bear their defiance and she meant to find out what she wanted to know.

But Nick wouldn't say anything more, and Katie, though she was close to tears, wouldn't give away the secret of the tree-house. In the end her aunt locked the bedroom doors again and went downstairs.

"No tea," groaned Nick. "I'm hungry, aren't you?"

"Laura will wonder what's happened to us," said Katie. "Listen! Surely that's Russet whining?"

She got out of bed and went to the window. Down below in the garden was Russet. Laura was at the front door, looking a little scared, for she was afraid of the children's aunt.

Aunt Margaret opened the door. "Please may I speak to Katie and Nick?" the children heard her ask in her clear voice.

"No. They're in disgrace," their aunt snapped. "They're in bed. They've taken things, and won't tell me where they've put them."

"What things?" asked Laura, after a pause. It was clear to the listening children that Laura guessed it was the things they had taken to the tree-house.

"Oh, never you mind," said Aunt Margaret. "You go home and tell your mother I don't want you to play with them any more. They're not to be trusted."

The door shut loudly. At once Nick called down to Laura in a low voice.

"Laura! I'm writing a note to you. Wait about a little, and I'll throw it down. I can't say much or Aunt will hear me."

Laura looked up and nodded. She walked off down the lane with Russet. Nick scribbled a hurried note, then felt in his pocket for something to weight it with. He found a big stone with a round hole in it, then looked out of the window.

He saw Laura coming back down the lane. He put the note through the hole in the stone, took careful aim and threw it. It landed neatly at her feet, which startled Russet! He growled and jumped back. Then he pounced on the note.

"No, Russet, no! That's for me," said Laura, and pushed him away. She opened the note and read it.

Dear Laura,
Aunt missed the clock and the picture, and because we wouldn't tell her where we had taken them, she's locked us up in our bedrooms. We've had no tea, and I don't expect we shall have any supper either! We'll come and see you as soon as we can. You'd better not come here again, in case Aunt tells your mother you mustn't play with us. Wasn't our day in the tree-house brilliant?
    Love from Katie and Nick.

Laura looked up at the window and waved. Then she set off down the lane with Russet. She ran almost all the way home. She burst into the kitchen where her mother was busy baking.

"Oh, Mummy, could you possibly give me some food for Nick and Katie?" she begged. "Please, please do! They may starve if I don't give them something."

"Good gracious!" said Mrs Greyling.

"The poor things! What's happened?"

Laura's mother was kind-hearted. Keeping a strict eye on Russet, who was standing on his hind legs trying to sniff at the new buns on the table, she made up a little parcel of biscuits and buns. "There you are," she said. "And don't you give any to that bad dog of yours, Laura!"

"Oh no, of course not," said Laura. "But he isn't a bad dog really, Mummy, only mischievous. He hasn't been very bad today."

"Hm! Hasn't he?" said her mother scornfully. "It wasn't Russet who took the sausages, I suppose? And it wasn't Russet who took the mat outside and chewed the ends off? And it wasn't Russet who got my knitting off the chair and ran off with it? Oh no, it must have been the cat!"

"Oh, I'm sorry. Did he really do all those things?" said Laura, upset. "He didn't tell me! He just comes in looking so good. Russet, why must you be so naughty?"

Russet put out a paw, but Laura wouldn't shake it.

"No," she said. "I don't shake hands with bad dogs. Only with good ones. I shall leave you at home now instead of taking you with me."

So naughty Russet was put in his kennel, and left there, whining, while Laura set off once more to Nick and Katie. She carried with her the bag of food.

Nick's room was at the side of the cottage. Taking great care not to walk in front of the windows in case Aunt Margaret should look out and see her, Laura crept under Nick's window.

She whistled. Nobody came. She whistled again. Still nobody came. She picked up a pebble, took careful aim, and threw it up to the window. Instead of rattling the pane it flew in through the opening at the top and landed on the wooden floor with a thud. Nick sat up, startled. He saw the stone and ran to the window.

"Shh!" called Laura, in a low voice. "I've brought you something. Open your window as wide as you can, and catch. I've got biscuits and buns for you. Tell Katie."

She threw the biscuits and buns up one by one and giggled as Nick managed to catch them. She had a good aim, and not one fell back into the garden. Then she threw Katie some. The children were delighted. They stood at the window eating and feeling very much better.

"I must go! I can hear your aunt," called Laura quietly, and ran off. Nick and Katie finished the rest of their buns and biscuits and got back into bed. They felt very much happier! The cakes were lovely, warm from the oven.

After a while their doors were opened and in came their aunt again. The children pretended to be asleep. They didn't want any more questions. They lay with their faces in their pillows. Their aunt was surprised. She had expected them to be hungry and sorry. She glanced round the room where Katie slept, and saw something on the floor. She bent to pick it up.

It was crumbs of cake! Aunt Margaret stared in amazement. "Cake!" she said aloud. "Now where did you get that from?"

Katie trembled. What bad luck to leave a crumb or two! Why hadn't she been more careful?

"Where did you get cake from?" demanded her aunt, shaking her, and making her turn round. But how could Katie or Nick give Laura away? Once again they said nothing, and once again their angry aunt marched downstairs, making up her mind that whatever happened she would find out these secrets! How dare they defy her like this? Well, she would show them what a mistake they were making – she would soon bring them to their senses!

CHAPTER 12

A PECULIAR SUNDAY

The next morning was horrible. Aunt Margaret meant to keep them in bed until they told her where they had put the picture and the clock. She took a miserable breakfast up to them, looking as black as thunder.

But Uncle Charlie, who was home for the day, because it was Sunday, had something to say about this punishment. He really was fond of the two children, and he liked them to be happy when they could. He was most astonished to find they were to be kept in their bedrooms all day.

"Well, I won't have it," he said, putting down the newspaper he always seemed to be reading. "What if they have taken the picture and the clock? It's just some childish game. After all, they were theirs. They weren't yours."

"How do I know they won't start taking

my things too?" cried Aunt Margaret, angry that her husband should take the children's side. "This sort of thing has got to be stopped. I won't have them growing up dishonest little thieves."

Uncle Charlie banged his hand on the table, and lost his temper, too. "I won't have you saying things like that! They won't grow up dishonest or bad. They're my only sister's children, and she brought them up well. They work hard and they don't grumble. They look after each other and their school reports are very good."

"Oh, I know you think they're perfect," said Aunt Margaret, "but they're not. They're bad and defiant and deceitful."

"That's not what their teachers say when I meet them," said Uncle Charlie. "They say they're two of the best children in the school. You've never tried to like them. You're a hard-hearted, spiteful woman!"

The children heard the angry voices and trembled in their bedrooms. It was dreadful to hear grown-ups quarrelling like that. Now what would happen?

Aunt Margaret was very angry indeed. She began to scold Uncle Charlie in a loud, never-ending voice, and he could hardly get a word in. In the end he got up and went upstairs. He unlocked the two bedroom doors and called to the children.

"You can come out. It's Sunday and I won't have you treated like this on that day, whatever you deserve on other days."

The children didn't very much want to come out and face Aunt Margaret, but they had to. They slipped downstairs, feeling scared.

"There'll be no lunch today!" said their aunt grimly. "I'm not going to cook for any of you!"

"Very well! We'll go out to lunch," said Uncle Charlie. Aunt Margaret said nothing. She was beaten this time, and knew it. But the children were sure she'd pay them back when she could. It didn't do to defeat Aunt Margaret.

They had lunch in the garden of a little pub with their uncle, after a long walk. He seemed sad and angry.

"I brought you to my home thinking I was doing the best thing for you," he said suddenly. "But I'd have done better to have let you go to a decent foster home. You would have been happier there."

"No, we wouldn't," said Katie at once. She had a great fear of being sent away to strangers. Uncle Charlie had his faults, but at least he was their uncle and was fond of them.

"Maybe Aunt Margaret will be happier now you have work again, Uncle," said Nick.

"Oh, I'll lose this job like I've lost all the others," said his uncle. "Don't you grow up like me, Nick. You work hard and do your best, as your mother did. I can't stand this life much longer. I'll have to get away and find work somewhere else."

"Oh no, Uncle!" cried Katie, scared. "Don't leave us. I couldn't bear to live alone with Aunt Margaret."

"Well, we'll see," said Uncle Charlie. Katie felt worried. Did Uncle Charlie really mean it? Perhaps he didn't. He'd threatened to leave before, but he never had. Supposing he did, though? What would happen to her and Nick, left alone with an aunt who'd never wanted them? It was a dreadful thought.

They walked back after lunch, and then

went to Laura's house. Laura was delighted to see them "Cheer up!" she said. "You look so miserable. Is your aunt still very cross?"

There wasn't time to go to the tree-house that afternoon, so they sat in the garden and told Laura all that had happened. Mrs Greyling brought them out a picnic tea.

"I think it's your aunt who ought to be punished, not you!" said Laura indignantly. "I wish I could come back with you and send her to bed and lock her in!"

"Woof," said Russet, agreeing. The others giggled. It was funny to imagine Laura locking their aunt in her room. Nick rolled on to his back, laughing. Russet went over and licked his nose vigorously.

"Oh, Russet, don't! Now I shall have to use my shirt to wipe off your lick," said Nick, sitting up. Russet put out a paw to shake. Nick eyed him sternly.

"Are you a good dog today, or not? Laura says we're not to shake paws with you unless you've been good."

"He has been fairly good, for him," said Laura. "He's only chewed up two things, my white socks and bit of my bedroom carpet."

"Well, I shall only shake one paw, not two," said Nick, as Russet held up his paw to shake. "You're fairly good, but not very good, Russet."

At last the children had to go home, though they dreaded it. "Still, Uncle Charlie may be home now," said Nick, cheering up. "Come on, Katie, I'll look after you."

They went back and stood outside the cottage to see how things were. To their relief, they found that Aunt Margaret had a friend in. She never scolded them when there was anyone there. She pretended to be kindly and sympathetic.

"Well, my dears," said Aunt Margaret, as they went in. "Did you have a nice time? I suppose you went to tea with Laura?"

"Yes, Aunt Margaret," said Nick. "We'd better go up to bed now, hadn't we?"

"There's some supper for you in the fridge," said his aunt, still in a gracious voice, put on for the benefit of her visitor. The children went to get their supper and ran thankfully up the stairs.

"What a bit of luck!" said Nick, sitting on Katie's bed to eat his supper. "I don't like Mrs Wilson very much, but I'm always pleased to see her here!"

"I do hope Uncle Charlie manages to get up at five o'clock tomorrow morning!" said Katie suddenly, feeling worried. "He hasn't got the clock to wake him now!"

"I'll try and wake him myself," said Nick. "Then tomorrow we'll fetch back the clock for him. I'd never have taken it if I'd known it would be wanted."

But, unfortunately, the next morning Nick didn't stir until the church clock struck seven o'clock.

Horrified, he jumped out of bed, hoping his uncle had woken in time. He peeped cautiously into his uncle's bedroom and saw him still asleep there. He called loudly.

"Uncle! Aunt! It's seven o'clock!"

They woke up, and Aunt Margaret leaped out of bed immediately. But even though he knew how late he was, Uncle Charlie wouldn't hurry. That was so like him. No wonder Aunt Margaret felt like shaking him, thought Nick.

Scolding and grumbling, Aunt Margaret got her husband out of the house, not letting him stop to have any breakfast.

Then she turned on the children.

"Now see what has happened! All because of you, your uncle has gone late to work. He'll lose his job if he does that!"

"It wasn't our fault," said Nick.

"Yes, it was. You stole that clock, just when I wanted it," raged his aunt.

"I didn't steal it, it was mine," said Nick. "I wanted to go and get it on Saturday but you locked me in my room. I'll go and get it today."

"You tell me where it is and I'll go and get it," said his aunt.

Nick was silent. Katie stared with wide eyes first at her brother, then at her aunt.

"Now, don't defy me again," said Aunt Margaret, looking grim. "You tell me where you've hidden it. That's all I want to know. Then if, as your uncle says, it's just a silly trick, I'll get it and say no more about it."

"I can't tell you where it is," said Nick. "It's a secret."

"How can it be a secret?" said his aunt. "Now you just tell me, or you'll be very sorry."

"I'll go and get it myself, Aunt, but I can't tell you where it is, because it's not only my secret," said Nick. "It's someone else's too."

"If you don't tell me where it is, you won't be allowed out of this house," said his aunt. "I'm not going to be defied by a boy of your age. Clear away and wash up, both of you, and when you've thought better of it, come and tell me what I want to know."

The children cleared away and washed up in silence. This was dreadful. They couldn't give away their secret, but how could they get the clock if Aunt Margaret wouldn't allow them to leave the house?

CHAPTER 13

A DREADFUL SHOCK

The next few days were miserable. The children didn't dare to disobey their aunt and go to the tree-house to fetch the clock, but how they longed to get away.

"It's too bad to think that we've got a wonderful place of our own, that nobody knows about, and yet we can't go and enjoy it," said Nick.

They had intended to ask Laura to fetch the clock for them, but she had told them she was going away for a few days to her grandparents.

The children missed Laura. If only she had been at home, she would have been able to talk to them over the fence, or they might have slipped out for five minutes to play with Russet.

Aunt Margaret was bad-tempered these days. She hardly spoke to them. She hardly spoke to Uncle Charlie either, but he didn't mind. She set Nick and Katie all kinds of jobs to do, and by the time Thursday came Nick and Katie had weeded the whole garden and painted the front gate.

On Tuesday morning Aunt Margaret had woken in time to get Uncle Charlie to work. But nobody had woken on Wednesday until half past seven, and the same happened on Thursday. Uncle Charlie didn't seem to care. He hated having to get up so early to get to the garage.

Then on Friday, Uncle Charlie came home and said he had lost his job again.

"Because you were late nearly every morning, I suppose," said Aunt Margaret, in her usual nagging voice. "Well, you can thank your precious nephew for that! He stole the clock so that you couldn't wake at the right time."

"You can't blame the boy for it," said Uncle Charlie. "He wanted to go and fetch the clock, wherever he had hidden it, but you wouldn't let him. You go about making things so difficult for all of us. I can't stand this atmosphere any more. I've got to get away."

"You've said that often enough before!"

said Aunt Margaret. "But you never do go. You'd rather stay and let me go out and work!"

"This time, I'm really going," said Uncle Charlie. "One of the men I work with has told me of a job up north. I'm going there. The money for the children is paid into the bank every three months by their Uncle Bob, and I'll send you money when I have it."

Katie was listening to all this with a scared look in her eyes. She flung herself on her uncle. "You're not to go! You're not to leave us! We don't want to be left with Aunt Margaret. Take us with you! We won't be any trouble, Uncle Charlie, really we won't!"

"I can't take you with me," said Uncle Charlie. "I know I oughtn't to leave you in this miserable place, but I must leave or I'll go mad. I want to make a fresh start and if things work out for me, I'll see what I can do for you. I'll write to your Uncle Bob and explain everything to him."

That was a dreadful weekend. Uncle Charlie packed his few things. Katie cried and cried. Even Nick had to blink back tears. Nobody could help liking Uncle Charlie, although he was irresponsible. Aunt Margaret either shouted or sulked. The children couldn't make out if she wanted their uncle to go or not.

On Monday he went, carrying a big bag with him. "Maybe you'll never see me again!" he said to Aunt Margaret, "and maybe it'll be a good thing for you if you don't. Take care of the children and treat them well, or as well as you know how. I'll send you what money I can."

The children went with him to the bus, Katie sobbing bitterly. He was the only one who loved them at all. It was dreadful to think that now they would be left behind with their Aunt Margaret.

Uncle Charlie got on the bus. It started off, and they waved goodbye. Still wiping her eyes, Katie took Nick's hand and they went back to the cottage, dreading seeing their aunt, and hearing her sharp tongue.

Aunt Margaret wasn't there when they went into the kitchen. They found a note on the table saying that she was catching a bus to the nearest town and would be back at teatime.

That evening she told them something that gave them a terrible shock.

"Well," she said, "I'm leaving too! I'm not living here with two bad children and working to keep them. As for your Uncle Charlie, he won't have any money to send. He won't find a good job, and he couldn't keep it if he did. So I'm off to live with my sister in Scotland and I've arranged for you to be taken into care."

Nick and Katie stared at Aunt Margaret in utter horror.

"No, Aunt, no!" cried Nick. "No! Don't do that. We'll be so good. We'll do everything you want us to. Uncle Charlie's going to write to Uncle Bob so that you'll get the money that he sends for us."

"Charlie won't remember to write without me there to remind him," said Aunt Margaret sharply. "Now, with him gone, I've got a chance to leave this place and make a better life for myself."

"Please don't go, Aunt Margaret," begged Katie, and actually went to her aunt and held her arm. "This is our home now; this is the place where our school and our friends are. What will happen to us if you leave? Where will we go? Oh, please stay here with us."

"You've brought it on yourselves," said Aunt Margaret, shaking off her hand. "I've been to talk to Social Services. A social worker is coming to see you tomorrow morning to decide what to do with you. I've said I want you away on Thursday. My sister is driving down to fetch me and I shall be staying with her. I'm letting this place to a friend of mine at the end of the week. I shall be really happy when I don't have to bother about a bad husband and two deceitful children any longer."

"Aunt Margaret, don't send us away," said Nick, looking very pale. "I don't quite know what would happen to us, but we don't want to go to strangers. We'd rather have a home here with you, even if we don't like each other very much. But if you'd be a bit kinder, we would try to love you. You don't seem to want us to like you even."

"I'm not arguing with you about what I'm going to do," said Aunt Margaret, slamming the oven door. "My mind is made up. I'm rid of your uncle, and I'll soon be rid of you too. You'll go on Thursday. And don't expect me to come and see you, because I won't!"

Katie fled upstairs, sobbing. Nick followed. They were both very shocked. Uncle Charlie had gone, and now they were both to go too. Nick put his arms round Katie, and they both wept together. Katie clung to Nick. He cried so seldom that it made things seem more terrible to see tears pouring down his cheeks.

"If only I was old enough to earn some money!" said Nick, wiping his tears away with the back of his hand. "Then I would make a home for you, Katie, and everything would be all right. It's awful to be a child and not be able to earn anything. I seem to be such a long time growing up."

Katie couldn't bear to see her brother's tears. She hugged him. "Don't cry," she said. "After all, we'll be together still. They do let brothers and sisters live together, don't they, Nick? Oh, Nick, I'm so unhappy."

"So am I, Katie," said Nick desperately. "More unhappy for you than I am for myself. And there's no one we can turn to."

"We must write to Uncle Bob at once,"

said Katie, wiping her eyes. "I know we can't go and live with him, but we must tell him what's happening to us, because I'm sure Uncle Charlie won't remember to write, and he doesn't know that Aunt Margaret is leaving us too."

"That's a good idea," said Nick, "though Australia is such a long way away. We'll write to Mike and Penny too. Their parents are kind and maybe they would keep in touch with us wherever we go."

"They always go away on holiday immediately school finishes," said Katie. "But their grandmother would forward our letter. Let's write this evening so we can catch the post tomorrow."

They bathed their red eyes and got out their writing things. Nick hated writing letters but he wrote to Uncle Bob explaining to him exactly what was happening to them. Katie wrote to Mike and Penny, who were in Spain.

"I kept imagining us on holiday with Mum and Dad while I was writing," said Katie, showing her letter to Nick. "That smudge was a tear that fell on the paper. Do you think I should rewrite it?"

"No," said Nick, giving her a hug. "I don't think they'll notice. Anyway, they'd understand how we're feeling, you know that."

The social worker was to arrive at ten o'clock the next morning. Aunt Margaret had made sure that the children looked clean and tidy.

"Now, mind you are polite and answer all her questions sensibly," she said. "If you don't behave yourselves when she comes, she won't bother with a family for you and you'll find yourselves in a children's home. She'll make the decision, not me."

"She wouldn't split us up, surely?" asked Nick. "Children aren't just split up and sent to anyone nowadays."

Katie was so horrified, she couldn't say anything. She was thankful that they had written letters to Mike and to Uncle Bob. Surely Uncle Bob would be able to find out where they were to be sent.

The front doorbell rang and Aunt Margaret took the social worker into the front room.

"I'm afraid I've only got half an hour," the children heard a loud voice say, "but first I need a few more details before I see the children."

Aunt Margaret shut the door of the front room firmly.

"She's put on her pleasant manner," said Nick. "She's going to make the social worker think she's a kindly person who really worries about us."

"I do hope she doesn't say horrid things," said Katie anxiously. "If the social worker is taken in by her, she'll believe everything Aunt says."

After ten minutes, Aunt Margaret came in with the social worker.

"Now, my dears, this is Pauline," said their aunt. "She's going to find somewhere for you to live as I can't look after you any more. Answer all her questions sensibly, and I'm sure she'll find you a nice home."

Pauline was a big, commanding woman. She looked the children up and down, then she spoke. "I am sorry to hear that your guardian has walked out and left you both," she said. "Your poor aunt is at her wits' end as to what to do with you, and I understand that you have no other relatives who can take you in."

"Poor children," said Aunt Margaret smoothly. "Their grandmother was badly hurt in the crash that killed their parents and will always need nursing care, and their great-aunt is in a wheelchair."

"We'll do our best for you, but it's such short notice that we won't be able to find you a long-term home immediately," said Pauline. "We shall have to put you in temporary care for the time being. I understand your aunt has to go to Scotland urgently to look after her sick sister. So I'll come for you on Thursday morning."

"What will happen to us?" asked Nick, hardly noticing that his aunt had lied to Pauline about her sister.

"We shall look for a foster family that will be able to care for both of you on a permanent basis," said Pauline. "On Thursday we might have to take you into a children's home for a few days, or to a temporary family."

"You won't split us up, will you?" asked Katie, her bottom lip trembling.

"I'm waiting to hear where we have spaces for you, but it's such short notice there is a possibility we may not be able to place you together immediately," answered Pauline, glancing quickly at her watch. "I'll be able to have a long chat with you on Thursday. I need to know all about you so that we can find the right family for you to live with eventually."

She asked Katie and Nick what they thought about going into care, but Katie was too miserable and frightened to say anything so Nick had to answer the question. He spoke as little as possible in case he said the wrong thing.

"We won't have to move away from the village, will we?" asked Nick. "We've only been here seven months and we've made new friends and we love it in the country."

"We wouldn't be able to find a foster family in any of these small villages," said Pauline. "Your foster family will probably live in a town – possibly somewhere like Swindon."

"You can't send us somewhere like that!" cried Nick. "I love the country. I love bird-watching and I want to become a naturalist."

"Now don't talk like that, dear," said Aunt Margaret, scowling at Nick behind

Pauline's back. "Beggars can't be choosers, you know."

"No point in worrying at present," said Pauline firmly. "You'll have to wait and see what we can find for you. Your aunt says that you're not always easy children to handle and so it may take a little time to find the right family."

"Aunt Margaret, how can you say that!" exploded Katie, tears running down her cheeks. "We do everything we can to help you."

"We'll talk again on Thursday," said Pauline. "I must go now and begin making arrangements for you. Goodbye, both of you."

Aunt Margaret took Pauline out into the hall. The children, looking at each other in despair, couldn't help hearing their aunt's parting remarks to Pauline:

"Of course they're both upset. But you must be careful. They can be very naughty. I haven't found them easy to look after."

Their aunt came back into the room. "I don't care where you go now," she said in a pleasanter voice. "I've got a lot of sorting out to do in the house today, so you can take sandwiches and do what you like. You can help me tomorrow and then pack in the evening ready for Pauline on Thursday morning."

They stared at Aunt Margaret in black despair. They couldn't believe it was true. How could Aunt Margaret do this to them? How could she lie about them? They went out to the gate with miserable faces.

"Let's go and see Russet and Laura and tell her we're going away," said Nick. "I'm sure Mrs Greyling will bring Laura to see us wherever we're sent."

"I don't want to go to a foster family," said Katie, her eyes spilling over with tears again. "I'm so frightened. I can't believe they might split us up even for a few days. I couldn't bear it."

"They may find somewhere for both of us, so don't worry yet," said Nick. "Let's go and see Laura and tell her what's happened. She was coming home today."

CHAPTER 14

IN THE MIDDLE OF THE NIGHT

Laura had just come back home. Her luggage was being unpacked, and she was running round the house and garden with Russet to see the hens, the bees and the goldfish in the pond.

"Aren't you glad that I'm back again?" Laura kept saying to Russet. "I'm really happy to see you. I did miss you."

Just then the two of them saw Nick and Katie coming up the drive. Laura rushed over to them, and Russet capered round in joy.

"Nick! Katie! How did you know I was back? Oh, I've missed you dreadfully! Have you been to the tree-house? I kept thinking of you sitting down in the little tree-room!"

Then Laura saw something in Nick and Katie's faces that alarmed her. She caught hold of Katie's hand.

"Something's happened, hasn't it? What

is it? Why do you look so sad? Quick, tell me!"

Nick told Laura everything. They sat down on a little shaded lawn, and Laura listened in dismay.

"But you can't go, you can't!" she said. "Just when we've got that lovely tree-house too! Oh, Nick, oh, Katie! This is the worst thing that could have happened! You're my best friends. You can't go!"

"We've got to," said Nick sadly. "We'll have to leave the lovely tree-house to you, Laura, and to Russet. You must go and play there, and tell us about it in letters. We shall be lonely and sad, away among strangers."

And then Laura's face suddenly brightened, and she cried out loudly, "I've got an idea! Oh, I've got such a wonderful idea!"

The others stared at her in surprise. Russet leaped to his feet and ran round excitedly.

"What do you mean? What idea can you possibly have?" asked Nick.

"You mustn't go off with that social worker!" cried Laura. "You must run away!"

"But where can we run to?" said Nick.

"Oh, how silly you are! To the tree-house, of course!" cried Laura, her face red and excited. "I'm sure that's why we discovered it! So that you could live there when this happened!"

"But – but – how could we live there?" said Nick, astonished.

"We could, we could!" shouted Katie, her eyes shining like stars. "Of course we could. Haven't we taken everything there? We could sleep there easily and nobody would know where we were!"

"They could hunt for weeks and not find you," said Laura, hardly able to speak for excitement.

"But what about food?" said Nick practically.

"I'll bring you some each day," said Laura. "And I'll take some money out of my money-box and buy you lots of tins of food in case I can't come every day. Oh, you'll have a wonderful time! Imagine living in the tree-house and sleeping there all night! It would be the most marvellous adventure in the world."

"We must go, Nick, we must!" cried

Katie, her heart beating fast at the thought. "We needn't go to strangers. We'll live in our lovely tree-house, and have Laura and Russet to visit us, and we'll be so happy!"

"I don't see how we can. People are sure to come looking for us," said Nick. "The Social Services will call the police out to hunt for us and we shall get into dreadful trouble."

"Oh, Nick, don't be silly! You can disappear quite easily with me to help you," said Laura. "And let people look for you! They'll never find you! I shan't say a word. It'll be a real adventure. Surely you're not going to say no to it?"

Nick didn't want to say no. The idea of going to live in the tree-house was so exciting, but was it right to get Katie involved, if they might end up in terrible trouble? He looked at the two excited girls.

"I don't think we'll be able to stay hidden for very long," he said, "but it'll give Uncle Bob time to get our letter and perhaps take some action to help us." He smiled. "Right, we will run away to the tree-house. We must plan carefully how we do it. We'll have to leave before Pauline arrives on Thursday morning."

"Oh, Nick! Thank you," said Katie, squeezing his arm. "It'll work out all right, I know it will, you just see."

"You said that your aunt told you you must pack your things tomorrow," said Laura. "Well, pack everything up and then tomorrow night take your bags, creep out of the house by moonlight and go straight to the tree-house!"

"What, in the middle of the night?" cried Katie in excitement. "Oh, Laura, what a marvellous idea! Will you be there too?"

"No, but I'll come the next day with lots of food," promised Laura. "I'd better not creep out and join you in your escape, because if anyone misses me that night they'll guess I've been with you, and it would be difficult not to give you away."

"Don't tell anyone you've seen us today, and don't come and see us tomorrow," said Nick. "Then no one will think you know anything about it. You'll come and see us each day once we've gone, won't you?"

Laura nodded, smiling happily.

"I'm so happy now that I can think sensibly again," said Katie, and she rolled over and played with Russet. "What a wonderful idea of yours, Laura! I was so miserable this morning and now I'm really excited!"

"Woof," said Russet, and gave her his paw.

"I'm sure he understands about it all," said Katie, shaking his paw. "Russet, you shall be the tree-house dog! Won't we have fun?"

"We'd better go now, before anyone knows we've been to see Laura," said Nick, getting up. "Come on, Katie. We'll pack our things tomorrow, Laura, and then, when the moon is up and we can see our way, we'll go to the wood, follow the string, and find the tree-house. We'll sleep there, and wait for you to come the next day."

"There are biscuits and chocolate there, and some lemonade," said Laura, remembering. "You can make that do for your breakfast. I'll bring what I can later. Goodbye and good luck!"

Feeling much happier, the two children went off home together. What an exciting secret they had now! Katie could hardly help dancing for joy.

"You'd better not look so happy, Katie," said Nick, with a grin. "Aunt Margaret will be certain that we're up to something if you look like that!"

"I can't help it," said Katie, trying to make her face solemn. But they needn't have worried. Their aunt was far too busy clearing up the cottage and putting things in the loft to bother about them or the look on their faces. She meant to leave on the Thursday too, and there was a lot to do.

On Wednesday, Aunt Margaret had them scurrying round helping to clean the house from top to bottom and iron the curtains that had been washed the day before. Nick and Katie were almost glad to be kept so busy until it was time to start their own packing.

"I hope you haven't packed anything of mine," said Aunt Margaret, who seemed determined to think they were not honest. "Katie, did you put your shoes in first, as I told you?"

"Yes, Aunt Margaret," said Katie meekly. She looked at her sour-faced aunt and was glad she was not going to live with her any more.

"Pauline will be here at nine o'clock tomorrow morning, and will take you away in her car," said Aunt Margaret. "I'm leaving for Scotland in the afternoon with my sister, as I told you. You can write to me if you like, but don't expect me to come and see you."

"No, Aunt Margaret," said Nick. "I hope you'll be happy at your sister's. Will you tell Uncle Charlie where we are so that he can come and see us sometimes, if he ever comes back?"

"Pauline will write to him and tell him where you're going," said Aunt Margaret. "He's your guardian, so he has to know. It'll be a shock for him. Serve him right for going off like that!"

"Why did you ask Aunt Margaret to let Uncle Charlie know we were going into care, so that he could come and see us?" whispered Katie, puzzled. "You know we won't be there."

"Of course. But supposing we're found, I'd like Uncle Charlie to know where we are, just in case Uncle Bob doesn't get our letter," whispered back Nick. "Don't look so alarmed, silly. I don't suppose we shall be found, but you never know!"

"What are you whispering about?" demanded Aunt Margaret. "You know that it's rude to whisper when other people are in the room."

Luckily she didn't insist on an answer, so the children said nothing. They kept on looking at the clock, longing for bedtime and for nightfall. Then their adventure would begin!

Bedtime did come at last. They said a polite goodnight to their aunt for the last time. She was ironing, and they heard the familiar *bump-bump-bump* of the iron as they lay in bed.

"You go to sleep, Katie," said Nick, in a low voice. "I'll keep awake. You needn't be afraid I shall oversleep!"

"Oh, Nick, it would be dreadful if you did, wouldn't it?" said Katie, thinking of the arrival of Pauline at nine o'clock the next day. "I feel worried in case you do, so I'll try to keep awake, too."

But she didn't manage to, and soon Nick heard her regular breathing as he lay in bed, waiting. He heard his aunt come upstairs to her bedroom. He heard the bed creak as she got into it. He lay still, looking out of the window and watching the moon coming up behind the trees. The church clock struck eleven.

The moon rose higher and cleared the trees. Nick's bedroom was brilliant with moonlight, but he waited until he heard the church clock strike twelve. Then he got up very softly, and padded into Katie's room.

He shook her gently. She woke up sleepily and rubbed her eyes. "Katie, it's time to go to the tree-house," whispered Nick, in her ear. "Don't make a sound! We mustn't wake Aunt, whatever we do."

In great excitement Katie got up very quietly and dressed herself. Her fingers were trembling so much that she had to leave half her buttons undone. But it didn't matter as long as they escaped to the tree-house in safety.

"Are you ready?" whispered Nick. "Then come on. Our bags are already by the back door."

They crept downstairs, holding their breath every time a stair creaked. At last they were in the moonlit kitchen.

They looked round the kitchen for the

last time. They hadn't been very happy in the cottage, yet they felt quite sad to leave it, knowing they would never come back.

They stole out of the back door, and closed it softly behind them. Then down the path to the lane they went, carrying their bags. No one saw them go. No one heard them. The big full moon shone down on the two figures hurrying away on their most desperate adventure yet.

They walked quickly to the wood.

Nobody was about at all. They meant to hide in the hedge if they saw anyone. A barn owl screeched and made them jump. A hedgehog scurried by in the ditch, and they wondered what it was.

They came to the wood and made their way to the part where the string began. "I hope we'll be able to find it all right," panted Nick. "It's dark among the trees. The moon's so bright tonight that it makes the shadows twice as black."

They came to the place where the string began. They felt about for it, and at last they found it.

"I'll go first and you keep close behind me," said Nick. "Your bag isn't too heavy, is it? I must have one hand for my bag and the other for the string, or I'd carry both bags."

"I'm all right," said Katie, her heart beating fast. "Go on. I want to get to our tree-house. I'll feel safe then. Walk on, Nick, quickly!"

They followed the string for a long way until at last they came to the little clearing beyond which was the great oak tree. How relieved they were!

CHAPTER 15

An Exciting Home

The old tree looked mysterious in the moonlit night. It was full of dark shadows, and it looked more enormous than it really was. It rose up, vast and black, flecked with silver moonbeams. Katie stopped to look.

"Come on, Katie," said Nick, setting down his bag. "Let's go to bed. I can't stop yawning, I'm so tired."

"To bed inside the tree-house!" said Katie joyfully. "No more horrid, unkind Aunt Margaret, no going into care; but instead the tree-house, Laura and Russet."

The children looked up at the tree, wondering if they could see how to climb it in the moonlight. Nick went up first, and then helped Katie. They left their bags on the ground, but Nick undid them and took out their night things. It wasn't any use bringing a toothbrush or flannel, because there was no water.

"How shall we wash while we're here?" said Katie. "We must wash sometimes, Nick!"

"Oh, we may find a stream or a pool," said Nick. "Let's go inside."

They found the rope that hung down the middle of the tree and, holding on to it, slid into the dark hollow.

"Wow! It's really dark this time!" said Katie, half scared. "Light the candle, Nick."

Nick felt for the mantelpiece and found the matches. He struck one and lit the candle. At once things became more cheerful, and the candle flame shone clearly, lighting up the little room.

"There's my picture on the wall," said Katie, pleased. "Your clock wants winding up, Nick. It's stopped."

"I'll wind it," said Nick, picking it up. He wound it and set it back on the mantelpiece. Its cheerful, loud ticking pleased them both.

They undressed and got into pyjamas and nightdress. Then they lay down together on the rugs and cushions.

"It's quite warm," said Nick, "we shan't need a covering. Katie, isn't it exciting to be here at night in the tree-house?"

"It's brilliant," said Katie. "Are you going to let the candle burn all night, Nick?"

"Only if you don't want to be left in the dark," said Nick.

"I'd like to be in the dark," said Katie. "It would make it more exciting."

Nick got up and blew out the candle. He felt his way back to the rugs.

"It's lovely, isn't it?" said Katie, with a happy sigh. "Oh, what's that noise, Nick?"

"An owl," said Nick, sleepily. "It can't come in here, and anyway it won't hurt you. Goodnight, Katie. Sleep well in our tree-house!"

Nick couldn't keep awake. He was soon sound asleep, but Katie lay awake, thinking. She fell asleep at last, and she and Nick slept peacefully all night through. Daylight came filtering down the hollow of the tree, and Nick awoke and sat up, yawning. He lit the candle on the mantelpiece and looked at the time.

"Wake up, Katie!" he said. "It's past eight o'clock! I guess Aunt Margaret's wondering where we can be! She'll be up now looking for us. What a nasty surprise she must have had!"

"Let's have biscuits and chocolate for breakfast," said Katie, beginning to dress. "Oh, Nick, isn't this fun!"

"We'll have to see if we can make a little window in the trunk of the tree," said Nick, dressing too. "I don't like doing everything by candlelight. I must ask Laura to bring a torch, in case we can't find the matches in the dark."

"Let's try to make a window after breakfast," said Katie, "and a curtain of moss and leaves. Here are the biscuits, Nick, and the chocolate."

"We'll go up the tree and have our breakfast," said Nick. "Come on. I want some fresh air. It's stuffy in here. Our bed wasn't very comfortable either. Later on we'll see if we can find some heather somewhere, and make a nice springy bed with it."

They climbed up to the broad branch, taking the chocolate and biscuits with them.

"The lemonade's in the cupboard, just near you," said Katie. So Nick got a bottle out of the hole, and unscrewed the top. It was a funny breakfast, but they enjoyed it. Everything looked fresh and new in the wood, and the children felt happy.

"When will Laura come?" asked Katie impatiently. "I want to tell her about last night."

They had to wait until eleven o'clock before Laura and Russet arrived. Laura had left immediately after breakfast, and had hurried as much as she could, but even so she couldn't get there sooner.

"Nick! Katie!" she called, as soon as she came in sight of the tree. "Are you there?"

They ran out from the trees, delighted to see Laura and Russet. Laura had her arms full, and had a bursting rucksack on her back, too. Russet once more carried a package which had slipped down under his tummy.

"Oh, you got here safely!" cried Laura, full of joy. "Great! I've brought you stacks of food. Help me get this off my back, Nick, it's terribly heavy."

Laura had certainly brought plenty of food. She unpacked two loaves of bread, some butter, cheese spread, peanut butter, jam, packets of biscuits, tins of meat and sardines, fruit and milk, and goodness know what besides! Nick and Katie stared in amazement.

"Enough to last you for ages!" said Laura. "I bought most of it with my own money, but Mummy gave me my picnic lunch and tea, and I made her give me a huge amount. Are you hungry? I bet you didn't find that biscuits and chocolate made a very lasting breakfast."

"They didn't," confessed Nick. "Let's have something to eat now, while I tell you what happened."

So they feasted on sardines and bread and butter, and Nick and Katie told her how they had run off in the moonlight. Laura had not been near their aunt's cottage so she did not know what had happened there when Aunt Margaret had discovered they were missing.

"Anyway, who cares?" she said. "We've got a perfectly lovely home for you, and I can bring all the food we want. Did you sleep well in the tree?"

"Yes," said Nick, "but our bed seemed a bit hard. We must try to find some heather to put under the rugs. That will make it softer. Russet, that's two whole sandwiches of mine you've had! Without even asking too! Are there any sardines left, Laura?"

"Two," said Laura. "Have them. Russet's a greedy pig. He had an enormous breakfast, because he ate the cat's as well as his own. Look out! He'll eat those sardines, too, if you don't watch him."

"It was a bit stuffy in the tree-house," said Nick. "We thought we'd try and make a window in the trunk."

"What a marvellous idea!" said Laura. She jumped up. "Let's do it at once. Then you won't have to keep lighting the candle."

They all went to the tree. Nick banged on it, round the trunk, up and down. It sounded hollow except in one place. Nick banged hard there and it felt softer than the rest.

"This piece is rotten," he said to the others. "I believe we could gouge out a hole here."

After a lot of banging and scraping and pushing, a big piece of the trunk fell away and dropped inside the tree. "There you are!" said Nick, delighted. "There's our window. Let's make it a bit bigger."

They managed to make a hole that was big enough to look out of. They couldn't make it any bigger, because round the window the tree was too solid.

Nick climbed down inside the tree, and grinned at the girls. They laughed. It was funny to see his face looking out through the hole. "It makes quite a difference to the room inside," said Nick. "It's quite light now, and it won't be nearly so hot. But we'll have to cover it somehow from the outside, in case anyone comes by and notices it. You never know if some rambler might walk past."

They pulled some ivy sprays loose from the tree trunk and draped them across the hole to hid the window. Anyone from inside could push them aside, or pull them across.

"There! A leafy curtain!" said Katie, pleased. "I guess we're the only people in the world who have a room in a tree, with a window in the trunk and a curtain made of leaves."

"It's very exciting," said Laura, laughing. And it certainly was!

CHAPTER 16

WHERE IS LAURA?

The children spent a very happy day indeed. They had plenty to eat and drink, the sun was warm, and there was always the big tree to go and sit in, or slip down inside.

"Let's see if we can find some heather for our beds tonight," said Nick, when teatime came. "There's some more string left, isn't there, Laura? We could use it so that we wouldn't get lost, and go a bit further into the wood."

So, unravelling the rest of the string, they set off to see if they could find a clear space where heather grew. But heather doesn't grow in the woods, so they were unlucky.

"Still, I know what we can use," said Nick, looking round the more open part of the wood where they were standing. "We can use bracken instead. We can strip off the tough stalks, and pile the fronds under our rugs. They would be nice and springy."

They wandered about, pulling at the bracken fronds, until Katie suddenly put her head on one side and listened.

"Surely I can hear water?" she said. The others listened too. They hurried to where the sound came from. Katie gave a cry of delight.

"A little stream going into a pool! Oh look, isn't it lovely?"

It was lovely. A clear stream bubbled from between the trees into a small round pool, which was fringed with rushes. The stream flowed out at the other end of the pool.

"This is our washing pool!" cried Katie. "I wondered where we could wash. Nick, let's do it now."

So they washed, without soap or flannel or towel, then ran around to dry off.

"This stream is very clear," said Nick, examining it. "I believe we could use the water for drinking."

"No, don't do that," said Laura. "Mum says water out of streams or rivers ought to be boiled. We've got a kettle and we could make a fire to boil water whenever we want to. Then we can have tea or cocoa to drink!"

"Good idea," said Katie. She sat down by the edge of the small green pool, and listened to the tinkling of the stream that flowed in and out of it. "This is fantastic. Now we have a house to live in, a pool to wash in and a stream to give us drinking water. Oh, Nick, we can live here for ever!"

Nick didn't see how they could possibly live in the woods in the cold winter-time, but he didn't say so, because the two girls looked so happy. Time enough to think of difficulties when they came.

Russet drank noisily from the pool. "It's funny that animals can drink from the dirtiest of puddles without getting ill," said Katie, watching him. "Oh, Russet, you've slipped in! Laura, get hold of him!"

Russet liked the pool. He waded about in it and then came out and shook himself so violently that hundreds of silvery drops flew all over the children.

"Russet, do that on the other side of the pool!" cried Laura. "You've got very bad manners."

"Woof," said Russet, and shook himself again.

"I'll have to go soon," said Laura with a sigh. "It takes a bit of time to get through the wood. It's a long way in, you know. I wish I could stay here with you and sleep in the tree-house. But if I asked Mummy, I'd be giving away your hiding-place."

"I wish you could stay with us, too," said Katie. "It's such fun sleeping inside a tree!"

"You're very lucky," said Laura. "Luckier than I am! Who'd believe that you live at Hollow Tree House in the heart of Faldham Wood. Amazing!"

For once in a way Katie too thought she was luckier than Laura. They walked back to the old tree, following the string. "I must go," said Laura sadly. "I really must. Mum will begin to worry about me if I don't. Goodbye. I'll come tomorrow and bring some more food."

Katie and Nick watched Laura go off with Russet, following the string. The sun was going down. It slanted between the trees, and the wood grew shadowy. A robin sang a little song somewhere.

"Let's climb up to the top of the tree

with a book and some supper," said Nick. "We can easily see to read up there. I'll get our books."

He swung himself up into the tree and down into the hollow. He found the books, and then went to the little window. He looked through it and called Katie.

"Hello, Katie! Here I am, peering out of the window!"

Katie looked, and laughed. She went to the window and tried to see inside the tree. It was dark, but she could just make out the things in the hollow room.

"I'll pull the curtain," said Katie, and dragged the leafy spray across to hide the window. She heard Nick scrambling up the tree to the wide branch, and climbed up to join him. They sat there, eating biscuits and reading their books in the last rays of the sun. The wind blew a little, and the leaves rustled and whispered.

They went down to bed when the sun disappeared. It was quite dark inside the tree, but not so stuffy as it usually was. "That's because we've got an open window!" said Nick, pleased.

Nick had lit the candle and the little

room looked cosy. They undressed, washed with some water in the old saucepan, dried themselves, and snuggled down on their bed which felt much softer with the bracken fronds underneath the rugs.

Nick blew the candle out, the little breeze cooled the hollow room and both children slept peacefully till quite late the next morning in spite of the light from the window.

"Hey, it's nearly nine o'clock," said Katie, waking with a start and peering through the window. "We must get up, Nick."

"No hurry," said Nick lazily. "Nothing to get up for till we want to. This bed is much more comfortable now."

Katie made him get up as she was hungry. They thought they would go to the pool and wash before they dressed properly.

"We might even bathe," said Nick. "Come on!"

They went up to the pool and stepped into the water. It was rather cold, but delicious. They dipped themselves right in, shouting and gasping. Then they dried themselves and ran to the little clearing, where the sun shone down warmly. They had their breakfast there.

"You know, we could make some more of those little baskets, from the rushes round our washing pool," said Nick. "We could give them to Laura, so that when her mother holds the sale in aid of the NSPCC next month, she'll have plenty to sell. That would be a little return for all the food Laura has brought. We can't pay for it in money, but we can pay for some of it that way."

"Oh yes!" said Katie eagerly. "That would be something to do, too. We'll get bored doing nothing all day long. What's the time now, Nick? Is it nearly time for Laura to come?"

"Yes, nearly," said Nick. "I don't think she can possibly get here before eleven o'clock. It's a quarter to now. We've just got time to go to the pool again and get some rushes to make baskets. Come on."

So off they went and soon collected a good supply of tough, narrow-bladed rushes. By the time they got back to the clearing, it was gone eleven.

They settled down to make the baskets

till Laura came. The time went on. Twelve o'clock came and no Laura. Half past twelve. No Laura.

Nick felt worried. What could be happening? Why hadn't Laura come? He hoped that her mother hadn't said she couldn't go out on her own. Usually, as long as Russet was with her, her mother didn't mind Laura spending the day picnicking somewhere.

One o'clock came. No Laura. "We'd better have our lunch," said Nick, who was feeling terribly hungry. "What shall we have?"

"Sardine sandwiches, bread and butter and jam, and some apricots out of a tin," said Katie at once. "There's no lemonade left. We'll boil some water and make some cocoa, shall we? We'll make enough for Laura, too, in case she comes."

Katie fetched some water from the stream, while Nick built a fire of twigs and lit it. The kettle was put on to boil, and blue smoke rose up, drifting away among the top of the trees.

"I wish Laura was here," said Katie, who missed her and Russet very much. "These are lovely sandwiches, aren't they, Nick? I seem to be much hungrier here than I was at Aunt Margaret's."

They ate a good lunch, and then made cocoa with the water out of the kettle, some tinned milk and cocoa-powder. It tasted delicious. They kept some in a jug for Laura.

"It's half past two," said Nick, looking worried. "Why doesn't Laura come, I wonder?"

Three o'clock came but still they were alone. At a quarter to four, when they had almost given her up, they heard the noise of someone coming, and they heard Russet's bark, too.

"Here they are!" cried Nick, and jumped to his feet. "Laura! Where have you been all this time?"

Laura appeared, with Russet at her heels. She carried more packages of food. She tried to smile at them, but to their horror, the smile broke in half, and her mouth went down. Big tears rolled down her cheeks, and a sob escaped her. Her eyes were red, and her face was tear-stained.

"Laura! What's the matter? What has

happened?" cried Katie in alarm, and ran to her friend. "Oh Laura, you look so dreadful. Do tell us what's the matter! Don't sob like that. Whatever can have happened?"

CHAPTER 17

RUSSET CHANGES HANDS

Laura couldn't say a word for some time. She was dreadfully upset, and poor Russet leaned against her, his melting brown eyes looking as if they would gush tears soon, too. His tail was right down.

Katie and Nick both put their arms round her. Katie was frightened. What could have made Laura so unhappy?

"It's Russet," she sobbed at last. "He's been so very naughty that Dad says he's got to go. He says he's got to go this evening."

"Oh, Laura!" cried Nick and Katie in dismay. "You can't let Russet go! What has he done?"

"He climbed on to the chair in Dad's study and chewed up a whole lot of papers on the desk," wept Laura. "He didn't know they were terribly important papers that Dad had been working on for months. He chewed them to bits. Then he was sick."

"Oh no!" said Nick. "How could he do such a dreadful thing? Laura, I'm sure your father didn't mean it when he said he was to go away. He's such a marvellous dog, and he's so gentle and funny. And surely your mother wouldn't let him go when he's your protector?"

"She will. She says Dad's right," said poor Laura. "She says she's given Russet hundreds and hundreds of chances, and he's getting worse instead of better. So tonight Dad is going to give him away to our old gardener. But he won't be kind to him, I know he won't."

"Oh, Laura – and you love him so," said Katie, with tears in her eyes.

"I do," said Laura. "You don't know how sweet he is: he licks me when I'm lonely, he snuggles up to me in bed at night and he looks up at me and almost smiles when we go off for a walk together."

Thinking of all the things that Russet did made Laura cry again. The others looked at her in despair. They knew how desolate she was feeling because they had had to give away Punch before they came to Aunt Margaret. Russet had helped them to get over their own misery. He was their firm and faithful friend. It was unthinkable that he was to go.

They all sat together, patting Russet and trying to comfort him for he seemed as upset as any of them. He looked up miserably out of sad dark eyes.

"You see, I shall never see him again if he goes to our old gardener, because he lives miles away now," said Laura despairingly. "Dad said I could give him to somebody else if I liked, but there's no one I know who'll take him and be kind to him."

The same thought struck Katie and Nick at the same moment. It was such a big thought that neither of them could speak for a minute. Then Nick, scarlet with excitement, blurted out what he had suddenly thought of.

"Laura! We'll have him! He's the tree-house dog, isn't he? Leave him with us, then you'll be able to see him every single day! He'll still be your dog, of course, but he won't live with you, that's all. He won't be able to sleep on your bed, but at any rate he'll see you every day, and you'll see him!"

Laura's eyes shone. Her tears stopped.

She gazed at Nick for a moment, and then she gave him such a bear-hug that he gasped. "Nick! That's the most wonderful idea in the world! Will you really have him here? Oh, isn't that marvellous? I can tell Dad I've done as he said, and given Russet away to friends."

"I was thinking of that, too," said Katie, and she hugged Russet. "Russet, it's all right. Don't look sad any more. You'll be with us, and you'll see Laura every day."

Russet's tail wagged and he rolled over onto his back with all four legs in the air.

"I think he understands. He's certainly pleased," said Nick. "But Russet, you have to learn to behave. You've made Laura very unhappy because she thought she was going to lose you."

Russet looked serious again. Laura rubbed her eyes hard with a dirty little hanky, which was quite wet through.

"Oh, I feel much happier now," she said. "Russet will be quite safe with you, even if he is naughty. I'll bring plenty of food for him each day."

"We kept some cocoa for you," said Katie.

"We built a fire and boiled a kettle. You have the cocoa, Laura. It will make you feel better. We'll boil the kettle again and make some more for all of us."

"I've brought some gorgeous fruitcake," said Laura, suddenly feeling hungry. "I didn't have any lunch at all, so let's have tea now. I couldn't come to you this morning because all the time I kept begging first Dad and then Mum to let me keep Russet."

"Poor old Laura," said Nick. He undid the package of food Laura had brought. There was tea enough for six people there!

"Chocolate biscuits, too!" said Katie. "Oooh, great!"

Laura had a little news of their Aunt Margaret to tell them. "Your aunt was furious when she found you had run away. At first she was just going to shut up the house and go to her sister's and not bother about you at all. But the social worker who came to fetch you yesterday said she couldn't do that. She said the police must be told and they would search for you."

"Gosh!" said Katie in alarm. "The police! I didn't think of them being called in."

"The social worker said you were too young to look after yourselves, and you'd have to be found," said Laura. "So your Aunt Margaret told the police. That's all I know."

"Oh dear!" groaned Katie. "I don't want people hunting for us. Do you think they'll come to the woods, Laura?"

"I should think so," said Laura. "They know you liked playing in them. Nobody has asked me any questions about you, which is lucky."

"We'll have to keep a good look-out, that's all," said Nick. "And we know that Russet will growl a warning if he hears someone."

"We'll have to slip down into the tree-house and hide if anyone comes," said Katie. "No one would think of looking for us there. We can keep very quiet. And we must remember to draw the curtain across the window!"

Laura felt rather sad when it was time to go home, because she had to leave Russet behind. He couldn't understand it. The other two held his collar firmly while Laura left. He whined and yelped and barked, and got very angry. But at last he understood that he was to stay with them.

"We'd better put him in the tree-house and block up his hole, in case he rushes after Laura," said Nick. "It would be dreadful if he ran back home and Laura's father found him and gave him away."

So they made Russet go in through his hole at the back of the tree, and then Nick stopped it up on the inside by placing one of their bags firmly across it.

"Sorry, Russet, but you'll have to stay put till you know that you mustn't run away," said Nick firmly. Russet was puzzled and cross about it, but he soon settled down, and fell asleep with his nose between his paws.

"Nobody has come to the woods to look for us today, anyway," said Nick, as he and Katie went down to the pool to wash themselves that evening. "I wonder if they will tomorrow. We'll have to keep a careful watch."

They went to the tree-house and slipped down into the cosy hollow as usual. It really did seem like home to them now. The clock ticked away on the funny ledge. The picture shone in the candlelight. Russet welcomed them, and made himself quite a nuisance, running round and round.

"Don't, Russet," said Katie. "There isn't room for gambollings and caperings in here. Now lie down like a good dog."

Russet crept over to them when they were lying half-asleep on the rugs. Soon he was safely cuddled into the bend of Nick's knees. Nick liked that. It reminded him of Punch.

"You feel so nice and warm there," he said. "Laura is going to miss you tonight though. Don't wriggle too much or you'll wake us. Goodnight, Katie. Goodnight, Russet."

There was silence in the tree-house except for the soft breathing of the three of them and the ticking of Nick's clock. They all slept soundly till the morning, and again a little breeze came in at the window and kept away the stuffiness.

Laura came the next day, looking quite happy again. "It's all right," she said. "I told Dad and Mum I'd given Russet to some children I knew and they didn't ask any questions. They just said they would give me a kitten. As if a kitten could possibly make up for a dog like Russet!"

Russet gave Laura an uproarious welcome. She might have been away for a year, the way he leaped around her and tried to lick every bit of her.

"He's been as good as gold," said Katie. "He hasn't tried to chew one single thing. And when we washed this morning he got into the pool and paddled. He's so sweet."

They had their lunch as usual in the little warm clearing. Suddenly, in the middle of it, Russet rose to his feet, and growled.

"What's the matter, silly?" said Laura. "There's nothing to growl at. Lie down and eat your bone."

"Russet doesn't growl at nothing," said Nick, looking puzzled. "Oh, no! I hope it isn't anyone coming through the woods!"

"Perhaps it's the police searching for us!" said Katie, going pale. "Oh, do you think it is?"

Everyone listened, but they could hear nothing except the wind in the trees and the laughing cry of a woodpecker. Russet laid down after a bit and stopped growling,

but he seemed to be listening all the time and wouldn't gnaw his bone any more.

The children went on with their picnic. Then suddenly Russet leaped to his feet again, and growled so fiercely that the children looked around in alarm. At the same time the sound of distant voices carried on the breeze.

"It is somebody!" cried Nick. "It *is*. I can hear their voices. It must be people hunting for us. Quick, we'd better all get into the tree, Russet too. I hope he won't growl like this all the time, or he'll give the game away."

They picked up their picnic things hurriedly, and made for the big oak tree. Up they went, found the rope, and let themselves down into the hollow. Russet came in through the back door, which was promptly barricaded by Nick, so that he couldn't get out. He was still growling.

"Now, we must all keep absolutely quiet," ordered Nick. "You too, Russet. Stop him growling, Laura. He mustn't be heard by anybody. I'm going to keep watch out of the window, and as soon as I see anyone I'll draw down the ivy sprays to hide it. Now, quiet!"

Russet stopped growling. The two girls huddled together on the rugs, hardly daring to breathe. The clock's ticking seemed very loud. Nick peeped out of the window.

The voices came nearer, and then Nick heard the sound of people making their way through the trees.

"They're coming," said Nick, and pulled the spray of leaves over the window. "Quiet, everyone."

CHAPTER 18

A NARROW ESCAPE

Through the window Nick had seen a group of men coming towards the tree. One of them was the village policeman whom he knew quite well. It was obvious they were searching the woods for Katie and himself.

"Hello! What's this?" cried one man, and held up Russet's bone. "A bone! How did that get here?"

"Some dog brought it, I expect," said another man. "The two children haven't a dog. It can't be anything to do with them."

"Here's the top of a lemonade bottle!" said another man. "That looks like children, doesn't it? I've a feeling they're hiding somewhere here. Separate and beat round for half a mile or so. Maybe we'll come across them. How they get food beats me! As far as we know they didn't take anything with them."

"Good thing we're tidy and didn't leave

our litter about," whispered Nick. He looked out through the window again, and then hurriedly dropped back on the rugs. "There's a man just outside! Don't make a sound."

Laura badly wanted to cough. She kept swallowing the cough down, and went almost purple in the face. Katie was trembling with fright and excitement. She held Nick's hand tightly. Nick was almost trembling, too. They were so near to the searchers, so very near!

The man outside leaned against the big oak tree, took his pipe out of his pocket, filled it with tobacco and began to light it, puffing hard. The smoke drifted in at the tree-window!

Laura wanted to cough again. Russet heard the man moving, and it was too much for him. He gave a low and fierce growl. The man stopped puffing at his pipe and looked round in surprise.

"Sounded like a dog!" he muttered. The children heard what he said, and gripped Russet hard. But Russet took no notice. He growled again.

"It's a funny thing," called the pipe-smoking man to another nearby. "I can hear a dog growling quite close by, but bless me if I can see one."

"You're imagining it," said the other man, with a laugh. "There's no dog around here!"

"Just listen," said the first man, standing up very straight. "That *is* a dog growling! Sounds as if it comes from this very tree!"

"You don't really think there's a dog shut in that tree, do you?" said the second man, laughing still. But he, too, looked puzzled when Russet's growl came again, sounding quite clear.

The children were in despair. They held Russet's mouth tightly shut, but he seemed to be able to growl in his throat without opening his mouth.

"Maybe there's a hollow in the tree," said the man. "It's big enough!"

The children heard this remark in the greatest horror. At any moment, the men would begin climbing up to see if the tree really was hollow!

Nick suddenly took hold of Russet and pushed him vigorously out of the hole, which was on the opposite side of the tree to where the men stood. Russet at once ran round the tree, bared his teeth at the two men, and growled so ferociously that they backed away in alarm.

"There's the dog, but he couldn't have been in any tree!" said the man with the pipe. "What a bad-tempered creature! Who does he belong to?"

"Don't know," said the other man. "Let's look at the name tag on his collar."

"Oh no! Now they'll find his address, and tell Dad, and he'll guess I must have given Russet to you. Then they'll know you're hiding near here," whispered Laura in despair.

But Russet would not allow the men to touch him. He growled again, and his white teeth looked so sharp that the men decided not to go near him.

"Come on," said the man with his pipe. "He's just wandered into the woods by himself, I reckon. Half wild, I should think, by his behaviour."

Russet didn't go with them when they left. He stood looking after them till they were out of sight, still growling angrily. Nick peeped out of the tree-window, and saw with relief that there was no one about.

"They're gone, for the moment," he whispered. "Laura, do you think you'd better slip home while it's safe? They've gone past here now, and you'll be able to get through the woods without being seen. You don't want to be questioned, because if you were you'd find it awfully difficult not to give us away. You can't tell lies about us."

"Okay, I'll go now, then," said Laura. "Phew, I was afraid Russet had given us away properly! I suppose it was impossible for him to stop growling when he knew our enemies were so near. It was a good idea of yours to push him out of the tree, Nick. That man really was about to discover our secret!"

"This is much too exciting," said Katie, who felt quite sick now that the men had gone. "Laura, do go before the men come back. We'll look out for you again tomorrow."

"I may not be able to come till teatime tomorrow," said Laura, climbing up the rope. "I've got one of my aunts coming to lunch, and I'm sure Mum won't let me go picnicking when she's there. Look out for me about four. Call Russet, Nick, or he'll follow me."

Nick whistled to Russet, very softly. Russet pushed his way in at the hole. Nick stopped up the hole, and looked out of the tree-window to watch Laura leave. "Good-bye!" he said. "See you tomorrow!"

Laura sped through the woods, following the string as usual. Nick sat down on the rug with Katie and Russet. It was fairly light in the tree, but not good enough for reading.

"Let's climb up into the branches of the tree with our books," said Katie. "We'll be able to see or hear if anyone comes near. Anyway, Russet will growl and warn us."

So up they went with their books, and spent a very pleasant time being rocked about in the boughs by the strong wind. It wasn't quite so warm as it had been, and big clouds were blowing up in the west.

"Looks like rain tomorrow," said Nick. "It'll be rather exciting being down in the tree-house with the rain pattering all around. We can play some games with Laura then."

When the searchers went back through

the wood they didn't go near the tree-house. Russet heard them and growled fiercely again, but they were not close enough to hear him. Nick saw two or three men in the distance, and he and Katie climbed very quickly and quietly down into the hollow. But nothing happened. No one came.

The next day dawned with a dark and overcast sky. A strong wind blew through the tree and the leaves rustled loudly. "I'm sure there's rain coming," said Nick, at lunch-time. "I hope Laura won't get caught in it."

Teatime came, but Laura hadn't arrived. "She may have been kept late," said Nick. "Perhaps she had to stay and see her aunt off."

They waited till five o'clock for Laura and then had their tea. They boiled some water to make cocoa as there was no lemonade left.

The rain began. It pattered loudly on the leaves of the trees. So Katie and Nick retired to the tree-house, lit the candle, and waited for Laura to come. But she didn't.

"I suppose she wasn't allowed to go out because it looked like rain," said Nick.

"Well, she'll be here tomorrow. Oh no! There's going to be a storm. That was thunder, wasn't it?"

It was. A great crash sounded almost overhead and then the rain came down even more heavily than before. One or two drops pattered down into the hollow tree and made Katie jump.

"One fell on my head!" she said. "Was that lightning?"

It was. It tore the sky in half, and lit up the inside of the tree far more brightly than twenty candles! Katie cuddled close to Nick. Neither of them was afraid of thunder, but it seemed rather scary to be sitting inside a tall hollow tree while thunder crashed outside and lightning lit up their room.

"I'm glad Laura didn't come," said Nick. "She might have been caught in this. I expect she didn't even start out."

But Laura had started out! She had set off about quarter to four, with a lovely tea for them all. She hadn't even thought about rain. She slipped off and ran to the woods. She found the string and began to follow it. But halfway to the tree-house, the string

181

had broken! Laura stared at the broken end in surprise. What had happened?

"I suppose those men broke it when they were hunting for Katie and Nick," she thought. "Bother! Now I must find the other broken end. It'll take me ages."

She didn't find it. It had slipped away into the bushes, and no matter how Laura hunted she couldn't find the rest of the string that would lead her safely to the tree-house.

"I'm sure I know the way without the string," said Laura to herself. "I've been this way often enough and it's not too far now."

So, very foolishly, she set off through the wood without the string to guide her. And very soon she knew she was lost!

She stood still in dismay. She didn't know which way to go. She was in a part of the wood where she had never been before. She looked at an old stump of a tree and knew she had definitely never seen it before.

"Now I'm quite lost," said Laura. "I mustn't get frightened. I'll try to make my way back."

So she turned herself around and went in another direction. Then something wet and cold fell on her head. The rain had started.

"I can't believe it!" said Laura. "Now I'll get soaked. I wish I had brought my jacket. I wish I was in the tree-house with Nick and Katie. But I'm lost, and the rain is getting worse and worse. The wood's getting so dark I can hardly see where I'm going."

Poor Laura! She wandered on and on, not knowing where she was going but hoping she would suddenly see the tree-house in front of her. Then the storm broke over the woods and she cowered down against a tree, listening to the rolls of thunder, and watching the brilliant lightning.

The storm went on for a long time. Laura was tired and wet and cold. She shivered. She was very miserable and longed for Russet.

"Russet!" she shouted. "Russet! Come to me! I'm shouting and whistling for you. Russet, I want you. I never get lost when I'm with you. Russet, Russet!"

But Russet was too far away to hear,

snuggled up in the tree-house. Laura called and called, and then wandered on again, so tired that her feet would hardly walk straight. She sneezed several times, and shivered.

"I'm getting cold," she said. Then she began to cry from fear and tiredness. "I want Russet! Russet, why don't you come and rescue me? I'm lost, and I want to be found."

But nobody came to rescue Laura. At last, tired out, she sank down under a bush, and her eyes closed. But all the time she talked in a little high voice. "Where's Russet? I do want Russet to come. Please won't someone come and find me? I'm so wet and cold. Russet, why won't you come?"

CHAPTER 19

AN ANXIOUS TIME

When Laura didn't come back that night, her mother and father were frantic with worry. They searched the house and the garden, but neither of them knew she had gone out to the woods.

"What has happened to Laura? Where can she be?" her mother said a hundred times. She kept going to the door to look for her.

"It's pouring with rain, and there's a storm blowing up. Did she take an anorak?" asked her father.

"No. I've looked. She disappeared after she said goodbye to my sister," said her mother. "She probably went to the woods as usual. She would have been by herself, now that Russet's gone."

"Good heavens! She shouldn't go wandering off alone in the woods without Russet," said Laura's anxious father. "She could easily get lost. I always felt she was safe when Russet was with her. He could be very fierce at times, and he adored her."

"I wish we hadn't got rid of him," said her mother. "I'm sure she must have gone to the woods. We'd better go and hunt for her there. Ask a couple of the neighbours to come too, and I'll telephone the village policeman and Mr Wilson, the forester. He knows the woods well."

The storm was directly overhead when the little party set off. They were all very concerned. Laura must have been caught somewhere in that dreadful storm. But where could she be?

They went into the wet woods. They followed this path and that path. They left the paths and hunted everywhere. They called and shouted, growing more and more despairing as the night went on. Each of them had a torch, and the beams gleamed on dripping wet trees and bushes.

Once the party came fairly near to the tree-house. Their shouts woke Russet, who was lying in the crook of Nick's knees. He raised his head and growled loudly.

Nick woke up. "What's the matter,

Russet? It's only the rain. Don't be silly."

Katie woke too. The children lay and listened to the pattering of raindrops all around, and now and again there was a plop as one fell into the hollow. It was cosy there inside the tree, listening to the rain and the now-distant thunder.

Russet heard shouts again and he leaped up and growled so fiercely that he almost frightened Katie. "What's the matter with him?" she said. "Be quiet, Russet. It's silly to growl at the rain."

"Listen and see if we can hear anything beyond the rain," said Nick. "Maybe it's someone lost in the wood."

But the rain drowned every other noise, and the two children heard nothing. They settled down again contentedly and went back to sleep.

Russet settled down, too. He couldn't hear the shouts any longer. The searchers had gone another way.

"Laura!" they shouted. "Laura! Where are you?" But no Laura answered. She was lost under a bush, shivering, soaking wet, half asleep and half awake, beginning to feel very ill.

And then at last, by pure chance, her father shone his torch down and saw Laura's foot sticking out from the bush! He stared in amazement, and then swung his torch so that he saw the huddled girl crouching under the bramble sprays. He gave a shout.

"I've found her, Marion. She's here. Come and help me with her."

Laura's mother came running, stumbling over the floor of the wood. The neighbours came, the policeman and Mr Wilson. They lifted Laura from her shelter, and looked at her. Her eyes were shut. She was delirious and didn't know what she was saying. She had caught a terrible chill and was shivering uncontrollably. She was very ill already.

"Poor child! She's wet through," said her mother, almost in tears. "Take off her wet clothes and wrap her in this warm coat. You carry her, Peter."

As quickly as they could they took Laura back home through the woods. Without the forester, they would have been lost themselves in the darkness. He knew every woodland track and guided them the right

way home, his torch shining steadily before them.

Laura was put to bed in the warm. The doctor was called out to see her. She had such a high fever that she didn't know what she was saying.

"She's been out in the rain, in all that storm, for hours and hours," said her mother, wiping away her tears. "All alone, too. How I wish we had never said Russet must go away. If he had been with her this would never have happened."

"Who is Russet?" said the doctor. "I notice she keeps saying his name."

"He was her dog," said her mother. "But he was such a bad dog we had to give him away. Laura was very fond of him, so I expect that's why she keeps talking about him now. But she doesn't know what she is saying. She keeps talking about Nick and Katie, too. Those are the two children who ran away, and they were her friends. People have been looking for them but they haven't been seen."

"It's a good thing you found Laura when you did," said the doctor, packing his things away in his bag. "She may be very ill tomorrow, possibly dangerously ill, I'm afraid. I'll be back in the morning to see how she is."

This was terrible news. Laura's mother didn't go to bed that night. She sat by Laura's bed, sponging her down with iced water while a fan blew cool air round her.

Nick and Katie would have been very worried if they had known what had happened to Laura. But they didn't. They wondered where she was the next day when she didn't come. They looked out for her all day long, and so did Russet. But there was no sign of her. Russet got so restless that Nick was afraid he would run off to find her. So he had to cut a piece from the rope that hung down the tree and tie Russet up to a small birch tree. Russet was angry. He barked loudly and whined piteously.

"I'm sorry," said Nick, patting him. "But if you did go back to Laura's house, you'd find yourself given away to someone you wouldn't like and Laura would never see you again. You must be patient."

The children went on with their basket-making, until they had a great many. They put them in one of the tree cupboards, stacked neatly on top of one another.

They read, sitting in the topmost branches of the big tree. They swam. They took Russet for a walk on the rope-lead, and he was as good as gold after a bit. He looked at them mournfully out of his big sad eyes, but he didn't try to run away.

When teatime came the two children gave Laura up. Nick was worried. "I simply can't think why she doesn't come," he said. "Do you suppose her mother has forbidden her to go for a walk without Russet?"

"Oh, I didn't think of that," said Katie, dismayed. "But surely she would come just once to tell us? What shall we do for food, if she doesn't come?"

"She's sure to come," said Nick, pretending to be far more certain than he felt. "We won't worry till tomorrow. It's a good thing we've got Russet for company, though I expect Laura is missing him dreadfully."

That day came to an end at last, and the children went to bed in the tree-house, feeling worried but hoping that things would be all right the next day.

"Perhaps Laura has had another relation

visiting her, or has had to go somewhere with her mother," said Nick as they settled down. "We'll see her tomorrow, I expect!"

But they didn't. The next day dragged on without any friendly Laura coming through the woods, bringing all kinds of delicious food. Their bread was eaten and so were their biscuits and cake. Now there was nothing left but half a pot of peanut butter and a few tins.

"This is getting serious," thought Nick, as he opened one of the tins. "Laura knows we'll soon be running short of food. I wonder if she's ill!"

Laura was very ill. She had a terrible cough, and such a high fever that she still didn't know what she was saying. She talked without ceasing of Russet.

"I want you, Russet," she said. "Why don't you come? Don't you love me any more? You know I'm lost and lonely, but you don't come. Where have you gone, Russet? Don't go away from me. Russet, where are you?"

Then her hands would feel over the bed for Russet, but he wasn't there. Her mother couldn't bear to hear her calling for the dog, and see her feeling for him.

"If only we knew where Russet was!" she said. "We've asked everyone in the village, but not a single child knows anything about him. Yet I'm sure Laura said she had given him to some children. If only we knew who he was with, I'd get him back for her."

"It would be wonderful if you could," said the doctor gravely. "It might save her life. She is so worried and anxious about this lost dog of hers that it's preventing her recovery."

Laura's mother wept. Russet was such a bad dog, but if only she could find him now, she felt she wouldn't mind what he did. It was a mystery, the way he had disappeared with no one knowing anything about him.

Laura's little high voice went on and on. "Russet, let's go for a walk, shall we? No, don't lick me all over! Russet, where are you? Oh, don't keep going away from me! Nick, Katie, what have you done with Russet? Have you hidden him in the tree-house?"

"What's this tree-house she's talking about?" asked the doctor. "If only she could answer our questions, but she doesn't even hear what we say. Where is this tree-house?"

Laura's mother didn't know. She couldn't ask Nick and Katie if they knew, either, because they had disappeared and no one knew where they were, although a search had been made for them over several days. Where could Russet be? If only they knew!

That night Laura was at her worst. She was so weak that she could hardly speak. But still she whispered about Russet and Nick and Katie, and the tree-house. She wouldn't have given the secret away if she had known what she was saying, but she didn't. Her mother held her hand anxiously and watched her.

The doctor came into the room and stood looking down at Laura, who tossed and turned on her pillows. "If only we could find this dog she worries about," he said, "she might have a chance. Where can he be? If we could get hold of him tonight, she might rally, but as it is, her anxiety is killing her. She'll have to go into hospital tomorrow if she's no better. How she must have loved that dog!"

Russet was far away in the tree-house with Nick and Katie. They, too, had had another anxious day, worrying about Laura. What could have happened to her? What was going to happen to them, too, when they had no more food? Would they have to give themselves up and go off in great disgrace to some foster family?

Nick sighed and tried to settle down to sleep. But Russet wouldn't let him. Russet would not go to sleep. Russet sat and howled as if his heart was breaking!

CHAPTER 20

RUSSET IS GOOD MEDICINE

Nick and Katie couldn't imagine what was wrong with Russet. "Why is he howling like that?" said Katie, stroking him and patting him. "Russet, don't! Have you got a pain?" Russet howled again, putting his head into the air and making a most piteous noise. "He's crying," said Katie, putting her arms round him. "He is, Nick. He's really crying. That's how dogs cry. He's crying for Laura."

"But why should he be so upset tonight?" said Nick, puzzled. "He didn't do this even on the very first night Laura left him here. It's only tonight he's so miserable."

Russet ran to the hole in the tree, but Nick had blocked it up so that he couldn't get out at night. The dog scraped hard, frantically trying to escape. He howled again and again.

"He wants to go to Laura," said Katie, pulling him back. "Nick, you don't suppose Laura is ill, or in danger, do you?"

"She could be ill," said Nick. "And that might be why she hasn't come to see us."

"Yes, I think you're right. She'd never have left Russet so long otherwise," said Katie. "And, oh, Nick, Russet knows it! He really does. Dogs know an awful lot without being told. He knows Laura wants him to go to her."

Nick couldn't help feeling Katie was right. They both knew that Russet adored Laura, and Laura loved Russet with all her heart. It might quite well be that Russet knew there was something wrong with Laura, and was trying to go to her.

Nick lit the candle and looked at the clock ticking away on the ledge. "It's half past ten," he said. "Dreadfully late. I don't know what to do. We can't let Russet go off by himself because if there's nothing wrong with Laura, he may be caught and given away. And if we go with him ourselves to find out what's happened, we may be caught!"

"Then we'd be given away too," said

Katie. "Whatever are we to do, Nick? I'm quite certain that Laura is really ill, and Russet knows he must go to her. But if seeing Russet would make Laura feel better, we ought not to worry about being caught ourselves. I think we'd better take Russet to Laura. If we didn't and anything happened to her, we'd never forgive ourselves."

"Yes, you're right," said Nick, giving Katie a hug. "We'll go now. It's dark, but we've got the torch Laura brought and we can follow the string easily enough. We'd better keep Russet on that bit of rope or he'll run off."

They blew out the candle, climbed up the tree, and went down to Russet's hole at the bottom of the trunk. Nick pushed away the bag he'd used to block the hole and let Russet out, but he held on to the bit of rope, to prevent Russet rushing off.

It was dark amongst the trees. Katie took Nick's hand, feeling a bit scared, and wishing there was a moon as there had been on the night they first came through the woods. Nick's torch shone steadily ahead. He found the string and began to run it through his fingers. Russet pulled at his lead and panted as if he had been running for miles. He seemed to know they were going to find Laura for he had stopped howling.

Suddenly Nick gave a cry of dismay. "The string is broken just here! Bother! I shall never find the other end in the dark!"

They looked all over the place, but they couldn't find where the string went on again. They looked at one another in despair. Russet whined.

"Nick, surely Russet would know the way and take us safely out of the woods?" said Katie suddenly. "Dogs know the way much better than we do. I'm sure Russet would know it without any string to guide him."

"Yes, of course he would," said Nick. "Go on, Russet, lead us, and we'll follow, but whatever you do, don't get lost tonight!"

Russet had no intention of getting lost. He could find the way blindfold as long as he had his nose to help him. He put it to the ground and eagerly led the way, panting again with excitement.

The children followed and, to their

relief, Russet took them safely out of the woods and on to the road they knew so well. Soon they were half running to Laura's house, pulled hard by the eager Russet. He gave little yelps of excitement as he went. He was near Laura! He would soon see her again.

He turned in at the gates and they all went up the drive. Russet led them straight to the front door. Now the children were in a fix. What should they do? You can't visit people at past midnight, and bang on the front door!

"There's a light on in Laura's bedroom!" whispered Katie, who knew which room Laura had. "Look. Up there. I wonder if she's awake."

Before they could do anything, the front door opened, and out came the doctor, who meant to go home and get some sleep. He walked straight into the two surprised children! He caught hold of them tightly, and Russet rushed straight past him into the house.

"Now, what's this?" he said sternly. "Whatever are you doing here at this time of night? I shall have to call the police!"

"Oh don't! Please let us go!" said Nick. "We only came to see Laura because we were afraid she was ill and now Russet's escaped. He's gone into the house!"

"Russet!" said the doctor, astonished. "Did you say Russet? Good heavens! Was that Russet shooting into the hall like that? Where did he come from? My word, we must get him before he goes off again. We must take him to Laura at once! You come along in. We've got to sort this out. Coming to the house at this time of night! Most peculiar."

He pulled Nick and Laura indoors. They were frightened. He took them into a study, where Laura's father sat, trying to read, anxious and sad. He stared in amazement at the two children.

"Do you know who these children are?" demanded the doctor. "I found them on your doorstep just now, complete with Russet, the dog we've wanted for days!"

"Russet! Is he back?" cried Laura's father, amazed. "Where is he?"

He was in the one place he longed to be: in Laura's bedroom. He had fled upstairs, and had made his way to his little mistress's

room. The door was ajar, and Russet put his nose to the crack, opening it a little wider. He could see Laura lying in bed.

With a joyful bark he flung himself across the room and on to the bed. He covered Laura's face with wet licks. He whined with happiness, and cuddled himself against her with the utmost joy.

Laura's eyes opened. She smiled a little for the first time since she had been ill. "Why, Russet!" she said. "Darling Russet! You've come at last. I thought you were lost. Don't leave me again, Russet."

Russet sensed that there was something

wrong with his beloved mistress. He stopped licking her. He stopped flinging himself about. He lay down quietly against her, giving a little whine of happiness now and again. Laura's hand found his head, and began to smooth down his long, droopy ears.

"I've missed you so," she said. "Stay with me, Russet."

Russet did stay with her. When Laura's mother and father and the doctor came to her room, she was fast asleep with Russet beside her. Laura had a smile on her face, and she looked better already.

"He's probably saved her life," said the doctor. "He came just in time to help her turn the corner. Leave him there. He'll be her best medicine now."

Russet wagged a polite tail at the company, but he didn't get off Laura's bed. He was sure that nobody would turn him off. He had found the person he loved best in the world, and that was all that mattered to him.

Mrs Greyling was crying. It seemed as if she could not stop. She tried to smile at the doctor through her tears.

He patted her arm. "Don't worry any more," he said. "She'll soon be well now. It was a miracle that the dog arrived this evening. Now, hadn't you better come along and see who came with the dog? Two frightened children who are very anxious to know about Laura!"

Mrs Greyling was surprised. She went downstairs with the doctor and her husband, and there, sitting on two chairs in the study, were Nick and Katie, rather white and very scared.

"Nick! Katie! How is it you're here?" asked Mrs Greyling in amazement. "Where have you been? Everyone's been hunting for you. And how was it you brought Russet with you?"

Katie began to cry. Mrs Greyling took her on her knee, and stroked her hair.

"Don't cry," she said. "I'm so happy tonight that I don't want anyone to cry. Laura was very very ill but now that she has got Russet back again, she'll soon be better."

"Oh, we wondered if she was ill, because she didn't come to the tree-house as she said she would!" said Katie.

"The tree-house! Laura kept talking about the tree-house," said the doctor. "What is it?"

The children said nothing for a minute. Then Nick spoke.

"Well, it's a secret really. But I suppose it won't be a secret any more. It's a house in a big old hollow tree. It belongs to me and Katie and Laura, and Russet, of course. We had such fun there."

"When we ran away we went to live there and Laura helped us and brought us food," said Katie, thinking that it couldn't possibly matter telling this to Mrs Greyling. "Then when Laura didn't come and didn't come, Russet became very miserable and tonight he began to howl. We thought he must know that there was something wrong with her so we brought him here."

"I'm very glad you did," said Mrs Greyling. "I haven't enough words to tell you how glad I am. We couldn't imagine where Russet had gone."

"You won't give him away, will you?" asked Katie anxiously. "It would break Laura's heart now that she's got him back again. She does love him so."

"I know," said Mr Greyling. "No, I won't give him away to anyone now. He'll stay with Laura, however naughty he is."

"What shall we do tonight?" asked Nick. "We don't know the way back to the tree-house because the guiding string is broken. So we—"

"As if I'd let you go back there tonight – and in the dark!" cried Mrs Greyling. She turned to her husband. "We must keep these children for a few days. We can't possibly hand them over to the social worker or to that dreadful aunt of theirs. We must see what can be done for them. Laura will love to have them with her as soon as she is well enough to sit up. This must be your home for a while!"

"Oh, thank you!" cried Katie, in joy. "There couldn't be anything nicer than that!"

CHAPTER 21

LAURA TELLS A STORY

It was marvellous to go to bed in Laura's home knowing that Laura was better and that Russet was with her. It was lovely to have Laura's mother coming to tuck them up and say goodnight to them.

"This is what I've missed," said Katie, smiling in delight. "It's almost like being back at our own home again. I know it's only for a few days, but it's wonderful."

The children were allowed to see Laura for a short time the next day. She was much better, but very weak, and tears sprang to her eyes almost every minute. She smiled at Nick and Katie. "Thank you for bringing Russet back," she whispered. "Even though you knew you might be caught, you still brought him back to me."

Nick and Katie were shocked to see the thin, white-faced Laura. Russet lay proudly on her bed, thumping his tail at them.

Laura's mother had told the police that the two children had been found, and that she was keeping them for a few days. She loved Katie, and she thought Nick was a fine boy, straight and truthful and kind. She liked the way he looked after Katie.

"They're two of the nicest children I've ever known," she told her husband. "If Laura had had a brother and a sister, I hope they would have been like Nick and Katie. I'm glad Laura made friends with them."

Her husband looked at her. "Yes," he said, "I think they would have made a good brother and sister for Laura too, and I don't see any reason why they shouldn't!"

"Why, what do you mean?" asked Laura's mother in surprise.

"Well, these children have no home now, and the one they had was a miserable one," said her husband. "Why can't we take these two children ourselves, give them a home and care for them? We can afford it and they would be like a brother and sister for Laura. Their aunt doesn't want them and their uncle isn't competent to care for them. He might be happy to agree to it."

Laura's mother thought about it for a

long time. Then she nodded her head. "Yes," she said, "I think you're right. These children deserve to have a chance of happiness, and we can give it to them. We'll have to get in touch with Social Services and the children's two guardians and discuss our suggestion with them. If it is possible for Nick and Katie to live with us, then we must talk it over with Laura."

That afternoon Sally Jones from Social Services came to see Mr and Mrs Greyling. She was very thankful that Nick and Katie had been found and listened carefully to the Greylings' idea of giving Nick and Katie a permanent home.

"It might be possible for you to foster them privately," Sally said, "but we have to take great care that the children go to the right family, especially at their age. We should have to talk to Nick and Katie and see what they really want. Their guardians would have to give their consent as well. There are a lot of inquiries that have to be made and forms to fill in which will all take time, but the children's welfare is our absolute priority."

"We quite understand that, Sally," said

Mr Greyling. "We've already talked to one of the children's guardians, their Uncle Bob, who lives in Australia. He was very worried after getting a letter from Nick. He said he would be happy for the children to live with us, if that's what they wanted. The other guardian is their Uncle Charlie, who walked out on the children last week. He heard they were missing and is coming to see them this evening."

"I'm going to talk to Nick and Katie about what they want," Sally continued, "and you'll have to discuss your idea with your daughter."

"I'm sure Laura would love the idea," said Mrs Greyling. "They are all such close friends."

"Before you talk to Laura, do think the whole idea over very carefully," warned Sally. "You must be quite certain that this is right for your family as well as for Nick and Katie."

"It might be preferable to consider adoption rather than fostering," said Mr Greyling. "Nick and Katie might feel more secure that way."

"Since you all know each other quite

well already, I can understand you might prefer a more permanent arrangement," said Sally thoughtfully. "An alternative would be a Residents' Order which would mean that you would take on parental responsibility for Nick and Katie just as if they were your own children. You have to apply to court for this Order to be granted. So obviously you would need to discuss it with your solicitor."

"Wouldn't it be a better idea to consider adoption?" asked Mr Greyling.

"I'm not sure that the children would necessarily want to be adopted," said Sally. "The Residents' Order gives you legal parental responsibility but allows the children to keep their own surname still. That can be very important to a child because it's a link with their real parents and their past. At the right time we can talk to them about it."

Sally went to see Nick and Katie after talking to Mr and Mrs Greyling.

"We've got to decide where you are going to live," she said. "I hope we'll find somewhere very nice for you both, but I'd like to know what you think about it."

"We must be together," said Katie, "and I'd like to be somewhere near Laura."

"I want to live in the country with a family who have a dog," said Nick. "But Pauline told us that it would be impossible to find a family like that near here."

"I'd like a family like Laura's," said Katie. "Mr and Mrs Greyling are so kind and I'd love to live with someone like Laura."

"I like people who laugh and are funny," said Nick. "Mr Greyling makes good jokes and I like talking to him – he's very interesting."

Sally asked a lot more questions, then she said, "I promise you I'll do my best to find you the right family and of course you'll stay together. Mr and Mrs Greyling are happy for you to live here for a while and I shall come back and see you in a day or two."

Sally said goodbye to them both and went to have a last word with Mr and Mrs Greyling.

"Think things over tonight before you decide to talk to Laura," she said. "Then talk to your solicitor, but don't say anything to Nick and Katie until I come back again."

While Nick and Katie were playing a game with Laura, who was still in bed, Uncle Charlie arrived. Mr and Mrs Greyling had a long talk with him and he was very pleased that Nick and Katie might be able to live with them. He gave his permission for them to stay with Laura until everything was settled.

Nick and Katie were delighted to see him, and were pleased he had rushed back to Faldham as soon as he'd heard that they had disappeared.

"I've got a good job and a little flat," he told them. "But your poor Aunt Margaret fell off a ladder at her sister's and has hurt her back."

"I hope she gets better soon," said Nick. "Uncle Charlie, we don't know what is going to happen to us. I suppose your job isn't good enough for us to go back with you, is it?"

"I'm sure the social worker will be able to find somewhere better to live than my flat in the middle of a town," Uncle Charlie said. "Don't worry, things will work out all right."

"Sally's kind and I hope she'll find somewhere nice for us," said Katie. "We'll write to you and you can visit us sometimes."

The next day Mr and Mrs Greyling woke up quite certain that they wanted to look after Nick and Katie permanently. So after the two children had gone off to the village, Laura's parents came into her bedroom to talk to her.

Laura was ecstatic when her mother and father suggested to her that Nick and Katie should come and live with them and be like her brother and sister. She could hardly believe her ears!

"Mum!" she said, almost pushing Russet off the bed in her excitement. "Do you mean it? Oh, I'd love it! Not having any brothers or sisters is the only thing I've ever been sad about."

"We can't tell them just yet as there are a lot of things we still have to discuss," said her father. "We'll wait until Sally comes back this afternoon."

"Oh, what will Nick and Katie say?" said Laura. "I can't wait to tell them!"

When Nick and Katie came back from

the village, they ran up to Laura's bedroom with a magazine for her. They went in quietly, smiles all over their faces, and were careful not to bump against the bed. Russet greeted them with a joyful bark.

"Hey, you do look excited, Laura," said Nick. "Has anything happened while we've been out?"

"Yes," said Laura, her eyes shining excitedly. "Something simply wonderful!"

"Oh, do tell us," said Katie. "You look so happy. You look almost well again!"

"I want to tell you a story," said Laura, quite forgetting what her mother had said to her.

"A true one, or a made-up one?" asked Katie.

"A true one," said Laura. "Listen.

"Once upon a time," she began, "there were two children who lived with a horrible aunt. They met a girl who had no brothers or sisters."

"It sounds like us and you," said Katie.

"Don't interrupt," said Laura. "Well, these three children became friends. They had a wonderful dog—"

"Called Russet," said Katie.

"And they made a secret house in a tree," said Laura. "And one day the two children ran away from their aunt, and went to live in the tree-house together."

"Why are you telling us a story about ourselves?" said Nick. "We know it all!"

"No, you don't. You don't know the ending," said Laura, "and I do. You wait!"

"What ending?" asked Katie, puzzled.

"Listen and you'll see," said Laura. "Well, the two children lived in the tree-house and the other girl brought them food, and left them her dog. Then one day the other girl fell ill, and she badly wanted her dog—"

"And the two children brought him," put in Katie, who seemed determined to tell the story too.

"Yes, and the girl got better, and everyone was glad," said Laura. "And the girl's mother said, 'This daughter of ours has no brother or sister. Why shouldn't we ask the two children to stay here always, and be like her brother and sister?' So they did stay, and they shared her mother and father and had a proper home again after all!"

There was silence. "That was a good

ending," said Nick. "A lovely one. But it's not a true one."

"It is, it is!" cried Laura. "Mum and Dad say you can live here with me, and share them and my home with me, if you'd like to. Would you like to? Your Uncle Charlie and Uncle Bob say you can, and Sally thinks it's a good idea too."

Nick and Katie stared at Laura. Share her family and her beautiful home?

"Is it true?" said Katie at last, in a funny low voice. "Is it *really* true?"

"Yes. I told you, this is a true story right to the end!" said Laura, laughing at them. "Oh, Nick, oh, Katie, think what fun we'll have together!"

Nick and Katie stared at one another, hardly able to believe that they were not going to be turned out and sent away to strangers.

"Oh, Nick!" said Katie, with happy tears spilling out of her eyes. "Oh, Nick! It's what I've longed for – a proper home again. How lovely to share Laura's mum and dad. We couldn't possibly have a nicer new family!"

Just at that moment Laura's parents

came in the room, and heard what Katie said.

"And I couldn't possibly have a nicer family than Laura, Nick and Katie!" said Mrs Greyling. "But Laura shouldn't have told you yet, because we haven't asked you if you would like to live with us."

"We should love to," said Nick, grinning all over his face. "I never imagined anything so marvellous could happen!"

"There's a lot to do before you can really belong to us," said Mr Greyling. "But we're all going to do our best and you'll have to be patient until everything's arranged."

"Your Uncle Bob and Uncle Charlie have agreed to everything and you'll stay here with us from now on," said Mrs Greyling. "Sally thinks it's a good idea too, and she's busy sorting everything out for us."

It was a very happy moment. They were all half laughing and half crying. Russet couldn't understand it. He held out his paw to Laura's mother, and she shook it. Then he held it out to Laura's father and he shook it. Then he held it out to Laura, and then to the other two.

"Russet thinks we ought to shake hands

on it!" said Laura, laughing. "Good dog! You'll like having Nick and Katie as well as me, won't you?"

"Woof," said Russet, and he thumped his tail on the bed. He gave Laura a very loving look.

"But he says he'll always love you best, Laura," said Katie, seeing the look.

"And you, Russet, are going to become a very good dog, aren't you?" said Nick. "There'll be three of us to take your training in hand from now on!"

"That's an excellent idea," said Mr Greyling, laughing. "I'm relying on you all to keep him under control until he's properly trained."

"You'll see!" said Nick. "He'll be the best-trained dog in Faldham by Christmas!"

"Woof! Woof!" said Russet, agreeing with him. And to Mr and Mrs Greyling's great surprise, so he was!

THE BARNEY MYSTERIES

Join Barney, Roger, Diana and Snubby
on their mystery-solving adventures!

ISBN 978-1-84135-728-7

ISBN 978-1-84135-729-4

ISBN 978-1-84135-730-0

ISBN 978-1-84135-731-7

ISBN 978-1-84135-732-4

ISBN 978-1-84135-733-1

Enid Blyton

THE ADVENTUROUS FOUR

Follow the adventures of Tom, twins Pippa
and Zoe, and their friend Andy who has a sailing
boat on which the four love to go exploring.

ISBN 978-1-84135-734-8

ISBN 978-1-84135-735-5

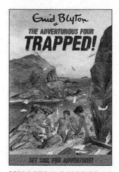

ISBN 978-1-84135-736-2

Enid Blyton

The Secret Series

Follow the adventures of Mike, Peggy and
Nora as they discover a secret island, explore
the heart of Africa and unravel the mysteries of
the Killimooin Mountains…

PB ISBN 978-1-84135-673-0
HB ISBN 978-1-84135-748-5

PB ISBN 978-1-84135-675-4
HB ISBN 978-1-84135-749-2

PB ISBN 978-1-84135-676-1
HB ISBN 978-1-84135-750-8

PB ISBN 978-1-84135-677-8
HB ISBN 978-1-84135-751-5

PB ISBN 978-1-84135-674-7
HB ISBN 978-1-84135-752-2

PB ISBN 978-1-84135-678-5
HB ISBN 978-1-84135-753-9

Enid Blyton

Enid Blyton was born in London in 1897. Her childhood was spent in Beckenham, Kent and as a child she began to write poems, stories and plays.

She trained as a teacher, but devoted most of her life to writing for children. Her first book was a collection of poems, published in 1922. In 1926 she began to write a weekly magazine for children called *Sunny Stories*, and it was here that many of her most popular stories and characters first appeared.

She wrote more than 700 books for children, many of which have been translated into over 30 languages.